Dear Luke,

I wish you were here. I really need to talk to you.

Today Miss Peters (my government teacher) stopped me after class and asked if I had thought of entering the speech contest for graduation. I told her I wasn't the sort of person who gave speeches but she said I should seriously think about it. I thought about it all the way home. At first I didn't think I'd have the nerve to do it, but the more I thought, the more it sounded like a good idea. Doing this speech would make everyone sit up and notice me.

By the time I got home, I was feeling all excited about the speech and dying to tell Chrissy. Then guess what—before I had a chance to tell her about it, Chrissy announced that she was entering the contest herself, and what's more, she wanted me to write her speech!

Help! I miss you so much.

Love, Cara

Other books in the **SUGAR & SPICE** series:

Janet Quin-Harkin's

Sugar & Spice

It's My Turn

Becky Thats what you are 1989 Love Pa Pa & Gram

IVY BOOKS • NEW YORK

Ivy Books
Published by Ballantine Books
Copyright © 1988 by Butterfield Press, Inc. & Janet Quin-Harkin

Produced by Butterfield Press, Inc.
133 Fifth Avenue
New York, New York 10003

Library of Congress Catalog Card Number: 87-92140

ISBN: 0-8041-0099-3

Manufactured in the United States of America

First Edition: August 1988

Chapter 1

"Aaahhhhhgggh!" Chrissy Madden let out a cry of horror so frightening that her cousin Caroline came rushing in from the kitchen with a half-eaten banana in one hand and a glass of milk in the other.

"What's the matter, Chrissy?" she demanded. Her face was pale and her blue eyes were opened wide, expecting to see a major disaster in the bedroom.

"Tammy Laudenschlager, that's the matter!" Chrissy said, looking up indignantly from the window seat where she was perched. She held up the letter she'd been reading.

"What?" Caroline asked. She shook her head as if she couldn't believe what she was hearing.

"I said Tammy Laudenschlager is the matter,"

Chrissy repeated slowly. "She's going to give the graduation speech at Danbury High."

Caroline looked from Chrissy to the letter and back again. "Chrissy," she said sweetly, "I came running in here, almost choking on my banana, because I thought that my cousin was in grave danger. I expected to find you at least wrapped in the coils of a boa constrictor, and it turns out that your very loud yell was only about a graduation speech?"

Chrissy grinned sheepishly. "So I tend to over do it sometimes," she said, "but that just made me explode. My mom was writing about all the graduation plans at home and I was sort of wishing I was there—so when I came to the part about Tammy giving the speech, I just flipped. It could have been me giving that speech, if I'd been there!" Chrissy said.

"But, Chrissy," Caroline said, looking amused. "You've never shown any inclination to give speeches. . . ."

"I know," Chrissy said, "but Tammy Laudenschlager is always wanting to be better than me. Remember how she tried to get Ben away from me?"

"I remember," Caroline said, taking a bite from her banana. "You solved that very nicely by pushing her into a blueberry pie. Thank heavens you aren't there right now or she'd have to stay away from dessert until after graduation!"

Chrissy giggled in spite of her indignation.

Caroline walked over and sat down beside her

cousin. "Come on, Chrissy," she said, "you didn't really want to give a graduation speech, did you? You're just upset because Tammy Whatsit is doing it."

"I guess," Chrissy agreed. "It just reminds me about all I'm missing. If I'd been able to stay home this year, I'd have been a big shot right now. Everyone would have known that I was graduating. All my relatives would have been there, and I might even have won an award or two. Here I'll be just one ordinary graduate among a thousand others. Nobody will care. . . ."

"I'll care," Caroline said. "I know it hasn't been easy for you to miss your senior year at home. If that tornado hadn't ruined your farm, you'd be back in Iowa right now. But your parents were right to have you stay here while they got the farm going again." She looked at her cousin's miserable face. "I think you've done very well to survive at a big city school like Maxwell, and even get accepted into college, Chrissy. You can feel proud of yourself."

"I guess," Chrissy said, "but I would like a little recognition, too, you know. I guess we're opposites that way. You don't seem to care if people know about all the things you do. But when Chrissy Madden does something, she wants the whole world to know about it."

"I've noticed," Caroline said. "Maybe you can wear one of your famous bikinis under your graduation gown?"

"Very funny," Chrissy replied. "I'd like to be

noticed for something positive for a change."

"You've been noticed a lot, Chrissy," Caroline said. "You've done a lot of good things since you came here. What about saving the park with the bulldozer? That got you noticed, didn't it? And what about when you were chairperson of the Senior Activities Committee? And dating hunks like Jeff, and now Bart? I'd say you've had more than your share of notice. . . ." Caroline's voice grew slightly wistful.

"I guess so," Chrissy said, nodding thoughtfully, "I know I've had a good education here in San Francisco and I've done things I'd never even dreamed about back home. You know me, I always get homesick when I read my mother's letters. It just seemed sad to be missing graduation back home, and all the things that go along with it—senior prom, parties . . ."

"But there are good things about to happen here, Chrissy," Caroline said. "Think of our senior ball."

"That's true," Chrissy admitted, immediately cheering up. "Our ball is going to be a heck of a lot more glamorous than the senior prom in Danbury. Listen to this," she opened the letter and found the passage: "I have been roped in again to make decorations for the senior prom, even though I don't have a senior at the high school this year. It seems I'm the only person who can make paper carnations that look like carnations and not like scrunched up paper! We're going to drape the whole ceiling of the gym with red and white paper flowers and turn the basketball hoops into giant red hearts! It should look real cute, I think. I'd rather be involved with the flowers than have to make dozens of little sandwiches for the refreshment table like Ben's mom is doing. In answer to your question, I don't know who he's taking yet. He was teasing Luke about the pair of them going together, but Luke said that no one could ever take Cara's place. . . ."

She glanced up at Caroline and smiled. Caroline blushed and a dreamy look came into her eyes. Ever since she had met Luke on a visit to Danbury last spring, she had not thought about anyone else. "I wish I could spirit him here for our senior ball," she said. "I don't think I want to go without him."

"You have to go," Chrissy insisted. "Everyone has to go to their senior ball!"

Caroline shrugged. "There are a few boys I could go with just as friends, but it wouldn't be the same. I'd feel funny dancing with anyone other than Luke."

"Oh, Cara, you're hopeless!" Chrissy exclaimed. "Just because Luke isn't here doesn't mean you can't have fun."

"What about you?" Caroline asked, wanting to change the subject. "Do you think you'll ask Bart? He would make a cute escort."

"Wouldn't he just?" Chrissy said, beaming as she pictured her new boyfriend in a tuxedo. "I hope the senior ball at the Forsythe School is on a different night than ours. Then Bart and I could go to both!" she exclaimed, but inside she felt a twinge of doubt. If Bart still likes me by then, she added to herself. He sure has been acting funny lately. She hid her thoughts from her cousin by smiling brightly. "Can you imagine sweeping into the ballroom of the Saint Francis Hotel in elegant evening gowns?"

"You see," Caroline said, getting up again, "there are things to look forward to here. And there's the senior trip, too. I bet your graduating class from Danbury isn't going to Disneyland for a night!"

Chrissy laughed, folding the letter as she did so. "It would be a week on the bus in both directions from Danbury," she said. "They usually have a senior picnic instead of a trip." Her laughing blue eyes were serious again. "You know, I guess compared to all the things I'd be missing here, I don't mind so much not being home for graduation. In fact, I don't know how I'll survive back in good old Iowa now that I've become a sophisticated city girl." She smoothed her long blond hair behind her ears and pointed her nose upward in what was meant to be a sophisticated gesture.

Caroline shook her head in amusement. "Are you having second thoughts about going to college back there?" she asked.

Chrissy nodded. "And third and fourth thoughts," she said. She shrugged her shoulders. "But it's all signed and sealed now, I suppose. I've been accepted at Iowa State and my family is all thrilled I'll be home again. I know in my heart that I should be home to help get the farm going again . . . but . . ."

"But?" Caroline asked.

"It isn't the sort of glamorous college other people are talking about," she said. "Look at you—you've been accepted to Berkeley and Colorado University!"

"But you've been wait-listed at Colorado, Chrissy. You might still get in," Caroline consoled her cousin.

"Fat chance," Chrissy replied. "You'll be having the time of your life in Colorado while I'm back in good, old Iowa."

Caroline leaned against the door frame. "Wouldn't it be heaven if Luke and I go to Colorado together?" She sighed. "But if they don't offer me some sort of scholarship, I'll have to choose Berkeley, I suppose."

"You could always work part-time," Chrissy said.

Caroline shook her head. "Not me," she said. "You know how long it takes me to get my homework done. I'm a compulsive perfectionist—see what big words I've learned in psychology class? I don't think I'd have the time or energy left for a job. I wish Colorado University didn't cost so much more than Berkeley."

"If you really want to go there, you'll find a way," Chrissy said. "It sounds like the neatest campus and just right for you, and to be with Luke . . ."

"I just hope things work out," Caroline said. "I've applied for so many scholarships. I wish just one of them would answer. Tracy already has two!"

"But Tracy's a real brain," Chrissy said. "And she wants to study math! Everyone's just looking for brainy girls who are math majors."

Caroline sighed. "I just wish more people were looking for ordinary girls who don't even know what they want to major in," she said with a little laugh.

"How about girls who just about scraped through high school," Chrissy reminded. "I was just praying I'd get into some college somewhere! I didn't even have the luxury of choice like you."

"Don't be such a pessimist, Chrissy," Caroline said. "That's not like you. Being wait-listed isn't the same as being rejected. Maybe Colorado is waiting for their first choice students to turn them down then they'll have a space for you."

"Thanks a lot," Chrissy said. "It's comforting to know that I'm everyone's last resort!"

Caroline smiled at her affectionately. "You are feeling down in the dumps today," she said. "I'll have to phone your mother and tell her not to write you any more letters about Tammy Whatsit. On second thought, how about I treat you to a sundae at Mama's? I've got to go over to James's house anyhow to talk about the class gift to the school. We're a terrible committee: I'd like to give a tree and someone else wants to give a microwave oven or a rock concert. I don't think we'll ever agree! The sundae will give me strength for the meeting. Coming?"

Chrissy leaped up. "Never let it be said that Chrissy Madden said no to a sundae," she said. "Let's have one big one between us and share—you get more nuts on it that way!" She draped her arm around Caroline's shoulder and hurried her down the hallway, just giving her time to put down her glass of milk as they passed the kitchen.

Chapter 2

"It feels like summer already," Caroline commented to her friends as they stretched out on the grass in the little park behind Maxwell High. She lay back contentedly, and gazed at the deep blue sky that provided the background for the pastel-colored buildings on the hillside. "It's so hot that Chrissy almost came to school in her bikini today!" she added.

"I did not!" Chrissy said indignantly.

"You did, too," Caroline said, laughing. "You had your bikini on and your book bag in your hand."

"You do exaggerate!" Chrissy said. "Just because I happened to try it on before school this morning did not mean that I was going to wear it out of the house. I had to see if I'd put on any weight over the winter."

The others laughed good-naturedly.

"Don't worry, Chrissy, you're still thin enough to slip down the plug hole in the bath if you're not careful," Maria said, glancing down at her own well-rounded figure.

"I wish I *had* decided to wear the bikini today," Chrissy said, propping herself up on her elbow to look at the others. "It was so hot in the physiology lab today, I thought my T-shirt would melt on my back."

Caroline looked at her with amusement. "I'm glad you decided not to!" she said. "I have a feeling that the sight of you in a bikini might have given some boys in physiology lab the idea for some hands-on experiments."

The others giggled again.

"Well, it's almost criminal making us go to school in weather like this," Chrissy said, her cheeks very pink with embarrassment. "They ought to close schools every time the sun shines."

"I agree," Randy said forcefully. "Let's take them to court for child abuse—making us study on a sunny day like this!"

"Oh, come on, Randy," said his girl friend, Justine, with a laugh. "If they let us skip school every day the sun shone in California, we wouldn't have learned much in our twelve years here."

"But we would have had a lot more fun,"

Randy answered, slipping an arm around her shoulder.

Justine gave him a little push. "Don't pretend you like being a flake," she said, "because we can all see through you. We know how excited you were when you got accepted by U.C. Santa Barbara."

"Only because it happens to be on the beach," Randy said, trying to defend his cool image.

"How do you put up with him?" Maria asked her friend.

"Oh, I only keep him around so I'll have someone to go to the senior ball with," Justine joked.

"There are plenty of guys who don't have dates for the ball, Justine," Tracy chimed in.

Randy snorted. "Yeah, a lot of nerds maybe. How about Brian Bennet? You could go with him."

"Oh no, he's got his eyes on Cara," Justine protested, giving Caroline a knowing look.

Caroline sighed. "Will you guys shut up about Brian Bennet! Just because we happen to be on the same committee . . ."

"But you must admit, Cara, that he follows you around like a puppy dog," Justine said. "It's so funny to watch you dodging into girls' rest rooms all over school to avoid him."

Caroline flushed. "He's not bad," she said hesitantly, "it's just that he tries too hard and he's . . . well, kind of boring."

"Kind of boring?" Maria exclaimed. "He's about

as exciting as Mr. O'Halloran's bookkeeping class."

The others all laughed.

"At least you'll have an attentive partner if you invite him to the ball," Tracy said. "That's more than I can say for George."

"Glad I don't have that problem with Dino," Maria remarked. "You always pretend that you don't like George but you keep going back to him."

"Chrissy's very quiet today," Tracy said, hastily changing the subject. "Are you coming down with something, Chrissy?"

"No, why?" Chrissy asked, looking up at Tracy as if she had been brought out of a trance.

"Because you are usually the noisiest person in the school," Tracy said.

"Me?" Chrissy asked, staring at them in amazement. "Quiet little me? I was just thinking that hardly anybody even knows I exist."

The others broke into noisy laughter again.

"Oh, come on, Chrissy," Randy said, leaning across to poke her in the ribs. "Who is the only person we know who can yell clear down the halls?"

"Maybe I did that when I first came here," Chrissy said, "but after two years, I think I've become pretty mature and sophisticated, like you guys . . . Will you all shut up laughing?"

"Is that why you were being quiet today?" Tracy went on. "Because you are working on your sophistication?"

"I think I know," Caroline suggested. "She's still brooding on the letter she got from home last night. She heard that her arch rival Tammy Whatsit, is going to be giving the valedictorian speech at graduation and it's made her depressed."

"Is that right, Chrissy?" Tracy asked.

"I guess so," Chrissy admitted.

"I wouldn't worry about it," Randy said in his usual flippant way. "After all, what's a speech to fifty people and three hundred pigs?"

"Randy, you are insensitive," Justine said. "Of course it means something to her. It's her own school and her own town. I can understand why she'd want to be back there. . . ."

Chrissy sat up, hugging her knees while she stared out across the blue waters of the San Francisco Bay, dotted with white sailboats. "I don't really want to be back there," she said, trying to picture the flat cornfields, the dusty roads, the white clapboard houses of Danbury. "I really like it here. I've had so much fun with all of you. It's just that it's almost over now and I'll be going back home and everybody will forget that I ever existed. . . ."

"Don't you believe it," Maria said with a big smile. "They'll be saying for years, 'remember that crazy girl? The one who drove a bulldozer down the street? The one that movie star Nick Matthews pulled out of the stream at Golden Gate Park?'"

"And who always yelled down the halls?" Randy added.

Usually Chrissy would have laughed along with them, but today she remained clammed up, still staring past them out across the Bay. Why was it so hard to explain to them how she felt?

"I know I've done crazy things while I've been here," she admitted, "but I think I've grown up a lot. I'd like to be remembered for something sensible too. I'd like to be noticed at graduation, the way I would have been at home. Here I'll just walk across the stage and go home and that will be that."

"The same for all of us," Caroline said. "In a school of three thousand, there just isn't room to notice everybody." She looked at her watch and got to her feet. "I have to run," she said. "I have a date with Brian Bennet at the Senior Gift Committee."

"Have fun," Tracy said, giving her a little wave as she turned to go.

Caroline looked back, making a despairing face. "Oh, great fun," she said. "We're hopelessly deadlocked. We've finally agreed on a picture for the entrance hall except that Steve Darby wants a free rock concert and every time I look up, Brian Bennet is gazing at me like a demented cow!"

She returned the wave and took off down the hill at a rapid pace.

"Poor old Cara," Justine said. "She always

seems to get herself on the most impossible committees."

"If that were me, I'd vote to give the school an extra month's vacation," Randy said. "That would be a popular choice with everyone."

"Which is why Cara was asked to be on the committee and not you," Justine answered. "Cara has worked so hard for this school. She deserves some recognition, but she's so quiet. She doesn't push herself forward enough."

"As she said, in a school of three thousand, it's pretty hard to get recognition," Maria said thoughtfully.

"After all, none of us is likely to be valedictorian," Tracy said.

"And Tammy Laudenschlager is going to be valedictorian back home," Chrissy said with a sigh. "I bet she got straight A's by bringing in apples for the teacher every day, because she sure wasn't the smartest person I've ever met! Now I'll always wonder if that could have been me standing up there on the podium saying, 'Ladies, gentlemen and fellow graduates . . . a funny thing happened to me on the way to the ceremony. . . .'"

"You could always compete for the senior speech if you feel strongly about it, Chrissy," Tracy said.

"The what?" Chrissy asked.

"The senior speech," Tracy explained. "Every year there's a competition to give a speech at graduation. The senior class votes on the best one."

"But isn't it always some outstanding student talking on the economy or splitting the atom?" Justine asked. "That's what I heard. They make the speech just prior to winning a Nobel Prize."

"But anybody can enter," Tracy said. "You can sign up in the government class."

"Chrissy could do a speech on 'Pigs I Have Known,'" Randy said, grinning at her.

"And I'll spotlight on you, Randy," Chrissy quipped back. Even in her current thoughtful mood, she was not going to let Randy get the better of her. There was more laughter.

"She got you there, Randy," Justine said. "I'd go for it, Chrissy. We need a lighter speech than the future of fossil fuel, heaven knows."

"I don't know," Chrissy said. "Maybe I'll think about it. I don't want to look like a fool against a lot of brilliant speeches."

"It depends on if you really want to go out with a bang or not," Tracy said. "I know that nothing in the world would make me get up in front of an entire auditorium and talk for ten minutes."

"It's bad enough getting up in front of the entire senior class," Maria added. "I hear they let you know very strongly when they don't like a speech or they think it's boring."

Randy got to his feet. "I don't know why we're sitting here discussing graduation speeches when we're about to be late for class," he said. "If we're not careful, we won't be wearing those cute little caps and gowns at all."

"Those caps and gowns look ridiculous anyway," Justine remarked. "They really are out of style."

Randy put a consoling arm around her shoulder. "Don't worry, my dear, I'll line up a designer to do a special cap and gown just for you. Who do you want? Bill Blass? Calvin Klein?"

They walked down the hill, laughing and talking. Chrissy brought up the rear of the group, still strangely silent. She watched the others uneasily, trying to work out why her middle felt as if butterflies in hiking boots were dancing around inside her.

It's not that I've got anything to worry about, she thought. *I've been accepted to college back home and I'm going to graduate soon and be back where I belong. My future is all secure and planned out, so why do I feel like this?* The answer came back to her almost immediately. *Maybe I'm scared because my future is all planned out. I'll be back to being little old Chrissy from the farm, just when I was almost a real California girl* ... She watched Justine and Randy jostling good-naturedly ahead of her. *Look at them,* she thought enviously. *They don't have a thing to worry about. They enjoy life, the way I used to. Just recently life seems to have become so serious! I have to go back home, whether I like it or not.*

She paused, checking her balance as they

reached a cross street while the hill plunged crazily down ahead of them. *But I want to go home, don't I?* she argued with herself. *I belong back there. I mattered there. I was somebody! Here I'm just a nobody—an ordinary student in school, but nobody important.*

Tracy looked back to her and smiled. "Come on, slow poke," she said. "We don't want to lose you on the way back."

Chrissy smiled back but her thoughts were still whirring inside her head. *I have lots of people who are nice to me here but sometimes I still get the impression they don't take me seriously! Even Cara got a laugh today telling about how I almost went out of the house in a bikini. Maybe I should try that speech! That would make them all sit up . . . and I'd love to see Tammy Laudenschlager's face when she hears that I'm making a speech not to a puny hundred people but to thousands!*

Her face lit up at the thought as she ran to catch up with Tracy and Maria.

Chapter 3

"To be or not to be an astronaut!" Chrissy exclaimed, lifting her arms dramatically. She observed the effect in the mirror and shook her head. "What do I know about astronauts? I even feel dizzy looking down from the top of a tall building."

It must be a subject I can talk about, she decided. *I can't talk on nuclear physics or even the situation in the Middle East. Now, let's think of things I do know something about. . . .*

She resumed her position and tried again. "'The Need for Conservation on the California Coastline,' by Christina Madden."

Again she shook her head. *There's no point in making a speech on that. All the kids at school are already for conservation. Besides, just tagging a few seals does not make me an expert.* She looked at her reflection critically, taking her long, blond hair and sweeping it up into a bun on top of her head. She reached out and put a pair of sunglasses on the end of her nose. "How I split the atom, by Doctor Christina Madden," she said out loud. "Well, it was easy. I just picked up a hammer, held the atom very steadily in place, and went wham!" As she said "Wham" she pounded the dresser, causing a lamp to go flying off the dressing table, taking with it the little silver dish in which Caroline kept barrettes, earrings and any other little knick-knacks.

"Whoops!" Chrissy said, kneeling to inspect the lamp. Luckily it was still in one piece and the bulb had not shattered. She was just putting it back in its place when she heard the front door slam.

"Chrissy? Are you home? Where are you—I've got something exciting to tell you!" Caroline's voice traveled down the hall.

Chrissy grinned. *Is this the same Caroline who used to walk down the hall so quietly that no one even knew she was home? Mama mia, now she yells as loudly as I do!* she thought.

"In the bedroom!" she called, scooping Caroline's things back into the dish. Before she could put them all back, Caroline had flung open the door and stood staring down at her with a questioning look on her face.

"Chrissy? What are you doing?" Caroline asked. "I thought I heard voices as I came up the steps. Is someone else here—and what are my barrettes doing all over the floor?"

Chrissy hastily picked up the last of the barrettes and put the dish back on the table. "I was just practicing in front of the mirror," she said.

"Practicing what, dare I ask?" Caroline said with a grin.

"My speech," Chrissy said. "Tracy and Maria and Justine told me about the senior speech contest and I thought I might enter it. Wouldn't it be great if I really won and got to make a speech at graduation? I can just see Tammy Laudenschlager's face when my mother mentions that I'm giving a speech to thousands of important people in a real auditorium, not just a crummy high-school gym!"

"You're thinking of entering the speech contest?" Caroline stammered.

"What's wrong with that?" Chrissy asked, her confidence suddenly taking a nose dive.

"Er . . . nothing, nothing at all, except that . . ."

"Except that what?" Chrissy demanded.

Caroline was clearly uncomfortable under Chrissy's questioning stare. "I just had no idea . . . you see, I didn't think—I mean, I didn't think you'd ever consider entering a contest like this."

"You thought I wouldn't have a chance of winning?" Chrissy asked. "Well, on my own I might not." She got to her feet and beamed excitedly at Caroline. "But with your help, Cara, I know I can do it. The speech will have to be fantastic to win, so I'm going to need all of your brain power, okay? I can put over a good delivery if I have the right things to say, so start thinking right now. I need a good topic."

"Chrissy," Caroline said, looking steadily at her cousin, "You take a lot for granted, you know. You always think that I'm going to help you with everything, even though I don't even have much time for myself." She paused, but her gaze didn't waver. "I helped you when you wanted to be in the school play, and I tried to help you to ski. I even taught you some ballet steps to impress Bart. But I don't remember you helping me very much."

"Of course not," Chrissy said, looking shocked. "You don't need help. You can do everything already. You already know how to behave and how to dance and the right thing to say ... besides, the one time I did decide to help you, by getting you together with a boy I thought you liked, you didn't appreciate it one bit."

"That's because you got the wrong boy, dummy," Caroline said with a smile. Then her face became serious again. "But had it occurred to you that I might want to enter this speech contest myself?" she asked.

Chrissy grinned. "I can't see you wanting to stand up in front of three thousand people. You—the famous human clam? Cara, I wouldn't put you through that. We'll make it a team effort, okay? You provide the great ideas and I'll deliver them to the world."

"And you get the credit for both?" Caroline asked evenly.

"Of course not," Chrissy said. "I'll do the sort of thing they do on the Oscars. You know, 'I want to thank my wonderful cousin Caroline for making today possible for me. Without her help and encouragement I'd never be standing here at this moment.' How's that? Is that good enough?"

"Have you thought that you have to win the contest first before you can do your sickening Oscars routine," Caroline asked. "What were you thinking of giving a speech on? It has to be something pretty special. 'My School Memories, by Chrissy Madden' is not going to do it."

"I know that," Chrissy said. "I have several ideas: I thought that maybe conservation might be a good thing, because I've been studying about saving whales in marine biology and I helped tag those seals last year. Or I could talk about preserving our heritage and bring in how we saved that park from turning into a parking lot!"

"But, Chrissy, I . . ." Caroline began, but Chrissy cut her off.

"I know—you're going to say that's probably too trivial and maybe you're right. It was only a little park. I need a bigger thing—a grander scale for a speech like this. That's why I need your great brain. Come up with a sizzling topic for me, Cara. You know the sort of thing—controversial, but not too controversial. Sexy, but not too sexy. Funny, but not too funny. Get the picture?"

"Oh sure," Caroline said dryly. "You want me to create the perfect speech for you in the spare time that I don't have. You're fine—you don't have to take two advanced placement exams in the next couple of weeks. All you have to do is keep breathing until you graduate."

Chrissy's face fell. "But I was relying on you, Cara. I don't want you to write the whole thing— just come up with the topic and get me started. Please, Cara . . . pretty please with sugar on top?" she begged. She put on what Caroline called her puppy dog face—the expression she used whenever she really wanted something. But for the first time it had no effect.

"You are a terrible con artist," Caroline said, pushing her away. "I'm going to get myself a snack right now and then I've got homework to do."

"But you will think about it, won't you, Cara?" Chrissy begged. "We cousins have got to stick together." She turned to watch Caroline walk away and the thought suddenly struck her. "By the way—what was it you wanted to tell me about? You were excited about something, weren't you? Was it good news?"

"It was nothing," Caroline said, not bothering to look around. "Nothing at all." As soon as Caroline was alone, she began to write to Luke.

Monday, May 4

Dear Luke,

I wish you were here. I really need to talk to

you. I'd love to call you, but the phone bill last month was enormous, so I'd better not. Instead I'll try to sort out my thoughts on paper. Get ready—this is going to be a long letter!

Today Miss Peters (my government teacher) stopped me after class and asked if I had thought of entering the speech contest for graduation. I told her I wasn't the sort of person who gave speeches but she said I should seriously think about it. She said that my name had come up several times in conversation in the teacher's lounge as being a suitable person to give the speech and she didn't think I'd have much competition this year. I thought about it all the way home. At first I didn't think I'd have the nerve to do it, but the more I thought, the more it sounded like a good idea. Can you imagine me giving a speech in front of lots of people—the same girl who ran away from an overly friendly cow at Chrissy's farm? (Remember that, Luke? How embarrassing!) But I've put in a lot of work for this school and yet I'm not one of the real popular people who get voted homecoming princess or anything like that. Doing this speech would make everyone sit up and notice me. I don't just want to be one of the crowd—especially not at graduation.

By the time I got home, I was feeling all excited about the speech and dying to tell Chrissy that Miss Peters thought I had a good chance of winning. Then guess what—before I had a chance to tell her about it, Chrissy announced that she was entering the contest herself, and what's more, she wanted me to write her speech! After that I couldn't seem to find the right time to tell her that I wanted to enter it, too. I did mention it once in passing but she made some joke about the way I clam up in public, so I just shut up after that.

Luke, what am I going to do? I don't want to get into a fight with Chrissy, but I'd really like to do that speech. It would be the one really special thing in high school that I could look back on when I'm old and gray. Of course, I know that Chrissy will try and talk me out of making the speech myself. She'll naturally want to do it instead, and knowing me, I'll probably give in to her. The trouble is that I've spent the last two years giving in to Chrissy most of the time. Now she's come to expect it as her right. In fact she takes far too much for granted—like I'll always help her with her homework, and lend her clothes, as if I'm just here to be a little genie she can conjure out of a bottle when she needs one. When she was telling me about her ideas for a speech, she even hinted she might talk about how she saved the park! That's a good laugh, because it was all my idea and my work. All she did was drive a crummy bulldozer, which naturally got all the publicity!

I wish I was the sort of person who could say what I'm feeling more, instead of keeping it all bottled up inside me! You're the only person I can really talk to who understands. As for Chrissy, she has been bugging me all year, but I can't say anything to her. It seems like it always has to be me who doesn't hurt Chrissy's feelings. When she first arrived, everyone expected me to help her out because she was new here. And this year everyone feels sorry for Chrissy because of the tornado. Don't get me wrong, I know it was horrible to have her family farm practically demolished, but the Maddens are just about recovered now, and I don't see why I should give in this time. It's my high school and I'd like the people here to remember me. I'm going to go ahead and enter the contest anyway. I'll face Chrissy when I have to—but I'm not looking forward to it!

Well Luke, that's about it for now. Thanks for listening. I think I'd explode if I didn't have you to talk to. I can't wait until next year when we're together at Colorado U. (with luck!)—absolute heaven! Take care, and have fun at all your graduation events. By the way, I don't mind if you invite someone to your prom just as friends. It would be a shame for you to miss it, so go and have a good time, and think of me.

Love, Cara

Chapter 4

The summery weather continued all week. At Maxwell High, the students gazed longingly out of the windows at the glorious California sunshine, daydreaming about the surf and sand while their teachers droned on about molecules and constitutions.

That weekend none of them needed any excuse to head straight for the beach. Dino's big van was crammed full of people, surfboards, wet suits and towels as it headed across the Golden Gate Bridge to the north, then wound over the mountain before dropping down to the bright blue waters of the Pacific Ocean. Unlike the real summer, when fog usually draped itself along the shore line, today the ocean sparkled, making the scene look like a travel poster for sunny

California. Dino turned the car into the parking lot and one by one the cramped occupants climbed down.

Chrissy stood among the pine trees lining the parking lot, sniffing the salty air with pleasure.

"Smells good, doesn't it?" Tracy asked.

Chrissy nodded. "I don't think I'll ever get over the smell of the ocean. I wish they'd find a way to put it in an air freshener so that I can sniff it occasionally back in Iowa! It makes you feel so free!"

Tracy stretched out her arms. "It makes me feel free just to be out of that van. I can't believe we squeezed in so many people."

"Yeah, it's a good thing Dino has a van, and not a little sports car like Bart," Chrissy remarked.

"A-ha! Bart the mysterious boyfriend," Tracy teased. "When are we finally going to meet him?"

"I don't know," Chrissy replied. "To tell you the truth, I haven't seen him in a little while. He really seems to have a great time when he's with me, but then a whole week might go by before he calls me again. I'd call him, but his mother doesn't like me very much. She doesn't think my family is rich enough or something. Anyway, I'm sure he'll call soon," she said with a confidence that she didn't feel. "Probably tonight."

"It is coming up to the busiest time of the year," Tracy remarked. "All the graduation stuff and advanced placement exams. Maybe he only has time to see you one day a week. I know I can't manage to go out more than that. I really should have stayed home to work on my chemistry today, but I just couldn't resist the beach—not on a gorgeous summery day like this."

Chrissy bent to pick up her beach bag. "I'm making the most of days like this. Soon I'll be back to exciting summer activities like helping with the hay or swimming in the creek," she said.

"They sound like fun things to do," Tracy commented.

"If you do them with the right person, right, Cara?" Chrissy asked as Caroline walked across to join them.

"I guess," Caroline said, and walked on.

"What's with her?" Tracy asked. "She's hardly said a word all afternoon. Is she worried about something?"

Chrissy frowned as she watched Caroline's retreating back. "I wish I knew," she said. "She's been kind of strange with me, too, as if she's trying hard to act normal but she doesn't feel normal inside."

"Maybe she's worrying about the exams," Tracy said, "Or maybe she's thinking about the senior ball. Tickets go on sale this week, you know, and she doesn't have a date."

"She has a date, but he's a thousand miles away," Chrissy corrected. "I hope she'll come anyway, or ask someone here to go. It wouldn't be the same without her."

"Are you going with Bart?" Tracy asked as they carried their things over the sand dunes to the smooth sandy beach. "Surely he'd be able to take time out for the ball."

"I haven't asked him yet," Chrissy said, "I sort of mentioned it once and he seemed to think it was a good idea. I'm sure he'll come," Chrissy said airily. "He's going to look so cool in a white tux. Maybe I'll get a turquoise-colored dress and he can wear a turquoise cummerbund and a turquoise carnation in his lapel . . . wowee! I can just see it now!" A big smile spread across her face.

"What's Chrissy grinning about?" Randy asked. He threw down a beach mat and stretched himself out on it. "She looks like the cat that ate the cream."

"She's daydreaming about the senior ball," Tracy said with a grin.

"Oh, the senior ball!" Justine exclaimed, leaning against Randy. "Tickets go on sale this week remember?"

"I don't see why I have to remember," Randy said. "I thought girls bought the tickets and boys bought the dinner and the limo and the corsage and everything else in the world."

"Girls have to buy expensive dresses, so that makes it even," Justine explained calmly, "and I've already said that we'll go halves on the limo."

"We can all take a limo together," Maria said, looking around at the group. "I wonder how many people they can fit into the biggest one? The cost won't be too bad if we share it. Let's see—there's Dino and me and Randy and you, and Tracy and George," she turned to Caroline and Chrissy, "and Chrissy and her mystery man, and Caroline and somebody . . . That makes ten.

Do you think we can get ten into one limo?"

"If we don't eat anything for a week in advance," Dino said, smiling fondly at Maria.

"Don't count me in," Caroline said, her cheeks flushing. "I don't think I'll be going."

"Oh, Cara! You have to come," Justine insisted, and everyone else chimed in.

"We'll find you a date," Randy volunteered.

"Er, no thanks," Caroline said, finally managing a laugh. "I know what your friends are like, Randy. And don't suggest Brian Bennet either! If I come, I want to select my own date—someone I can be comfortable with."

"Well, you'd better hurry up," Maria told her, "or all the good guys will be snapped up."

"Maybe I can find you a friend of Bart's from Forsythe," Chrissy suggested.

"No thanks," Caroline replied. "Like I said, I'd rather find my own date."

"Oh, okay," Chrissy said, stung by her cousin's abrupt answer.

"So we finally get to meet the fabulous Bart?" Maria asked. "I can't wait. I've never met anyone from a prep school before. I was beginning to think he was all a creation of Chrissy's imagination."

"Oh no, he's very real, trust me," Chrissy said, with a big smile. "And very, very cute. You'll all be totally jealous when you see him. When we walk into the Saint Francis Hotel together, every head is going to turn."

"Why, are you going to be wearing your bikini

again?" Randy asked, grinning at Chrissy.

"Oh shut up," Chrissy said, scooping up a handful of sand to throw at him.

"And speaking of bikinis, who's coming to get changed?" Maria asked, picking up her beach bag.

"I've already got mine on," Chrissy said, wriggling out of her shorts.

"Naturally," Justine said, getting ready to follow Maria. "I think you live in that bikini. Coming, Cara?"

"Thanks, but not right now," Caroline said. "I think I'll just lie here and read."

"You're not still working on that AP English exam?" Justine asked in horror.

"No—something else," Caroline said. "I need to get some ideas. You guys go ahead."

Chrissy squatted down beside Caroline. "Are you thinking of ideas for my speech, Cara?" she asked.

"What speech?" Randy asked as he brought his wet suit out of the bag and spread it out on the mat.

"The senior speech. I'm thinking of entering . . . and don't laugh," she added, watching Randy's face. "I don't think it's so funny. You wait until I give my famous speech on how I split the atom!"

She turned and stalked away, hearing Randy and Dino's laughter behind her. She walked down the hard sand of the beach, not looking back at the group.

Funny, but she had never minded being teased before she came here. Her brothers had teased her all the time, so had Ben and her friends back home. But here she did mind. Back home she knew she was pretty and smart and popular, but here in California she often felt that she had to prove that she was at least as good as the others.

I'll show them all, she muttered to herself. *Just wait until I win that speech contest. Then they'll have to be impressed. And what about when I show up at the senior ball with Bart? We'll be the best looking couple there. Nobody will think I'm just a little hick farm girl when I get out of his white sports car and sweep into the ballroom with him! I'd better hurry up and ask him if I've got to buy the tickets this week.*

She paused and looked out across the broad expanse of sand. There were already quite a few surfers in the ocean, braving the cold water with wet suits on. Her gaze drifted across the sand to a volleyball game being played up near the sand dunes. *Those kids make the game look so easy. I guess volleyball is just one of the many things I haven't managed to do so well since I've been here,* Chrissy thought as she recalled the bruises she'd gotten the last time she'd tried to play volleyball. *What's wrong with me today?* she wondered. *The sun is shining, I've nothing to do but work on my tan and be with my friends. I should be perfectly happy. I guess it must be end-of-year gloom. I've lived in San Francisco nearly two years now, but I don't feel as if I've made the most of it. Something's lacking.* She gave a determined sigh. *All the more reason to go out with a big splash! I wonder if that really is my speech Cara is working on. With her help, I'm sure to win the competition.*

As these thoughts went through her head, Chrissy walked past the volleyball game and began to climb. The dunes rose impressively high at one end of the beach—great mounds of glistening white sand dotted with clumps of coarse grass and hopeful creeping plants. Here and there were bright splashes of color where spring flowers had rooted themselves in sheltered hollows. Up and up she climbed, feeling the tug of the slope on her calf muscles. It was hot work, but she felt the need to be away from it all, to stand up on top of the highest dune and look down on the people on the beach.

I think I need some space to myself right now, she thought. *Maybe Cara feels the same. Maybe that's why she's so uptight this week. . . .*

She reached the top of the dune and stood, panting and flushed as she looked down. Her friends on the beach, the surfers in the ocean, even the volleyball players, all looked very small now, like insects in a sandy flower bed. She felt the wind in her hair and smiled as she swept her gaze along the beach.

That's better, she said to herself. *Now that I've got some good fresh air in my lungs I can think straight again . . . and I know I'm just as good as any of them. I'm going to work on that speech like crazy until it's the very best and it won't just be a crummy, country-girl speech, either. I'll show them that Chrissy Madden can be as slick and sophisticated as the rest of them!*

She turned and began to run along the top of the ridge, almost stumbling into a group of people gathered in a slight dip in the dune. As she checked her stride, she saw, perched on the sand, the biggest, most beautiful kite she had ever seen. It had blue and red wings stretching out on either side like a bird's, and a shiny metal frame between them. The kite sat there on the dune as if begging to be flown. Entranced, Chrissy walked up to it.

"Wow, what a huge kite," she said to the boys standing next to it. "I've never seen one this big! Is it really light enough to fly?"

She lifted it from the ground. It was very light.

"Hey, that's not a kite," one of the boys called, walking hastily toward her, "it's a hang glider . . ." But before he'd gotten the words out, a gust of wind blew up behind Chrissy, propelling her forward with the glider.

"Whoa!" Chrissy yelled, feeling herself driven by the wind. She began to run, trying to pull the glider back to earth, tugging at the metal bar as she fought to keep her balance. Suddenly the dune plunged downward—but Chrissy didn't. "Holy cow!" she yelled as she soared into the air with the glider. "How do you stop this thing?" she shouted, peering down at the horrified upturned faces of the boys as they ran to keep up with her.

Her arms felt as if they were about to be jerked out of their sockets, and she clutched the metal bar so tightly that her knuckles were completely white, but she didn't dare let go. The ground was alarmingly far away.

As the wind dropped, she was grateful to see the sand coming to meet her again. *Why do these things always happen to me?* she wondered, calmer now that it seemed the danger was over. *How was I to know?* She peered down to see the volleyball players scatter as her shadow darkened the sand. Parents scooped up their babies and ran out of her way, while everyone else on the beach stared up at her in amazement. The scene could have come straight from a movie. *So this is how Superman feels!* she thought.

The owners of the hang glider were drawing level with her, trying to grab at her trailing legs, and shouting out instructions she couldn't quite hear. The beach was just a few feet beneath her toes, then a few inches. Chrissy considered letting go of the glider, but decided to hold on, as several hands reached up to pull her to safety.

"Whoa!" she cried again as another gust shot her forward, causing the sunbathers in her path to fling themselves to the ground as she passed over them. "Help!" she shouted. "Watch out!" as she sent an umbrella flying and caught her foot in a beach chair, which she now dragged along behind her making an embarrassing clanking noise. The ocean was dangerously close. She began to panic. What if the wind lifted her up again and dropped her out to sea? Chrissy knew this stretch of coast was famous for its cruising sharks, as well as its dangerous currents. "Help!" she yelled again.

"Chrissy!" voices were shouting. Her friends' surprised faces flashed past her and she saw them race after the glider. At last they were just below her. With a mighty leap Randy reached up and grasped Chrissy's foot in his hands as if he were catching a touchdown pass. Then the rest of them joined in, until they had pulled Chrissy to the ground only a few yards from the ocean's edge.

"Chrissy? Are you okay?" They clustered around her. "Chrissy? What on earth were you trying to do? You don't know how to hang-glide. You might have killed yourself."

"Honestly, Chrissy, sometimes I wonder about you," Tracy said, shaking her head and smiling at the same time. "I don't believe anyone has ever done as many crazy things as you!"

"She can't be left alone for a minute," Maria added, smiling at her fondly.

"It was just an accident," Chrissy said, blushing scarlet in embarrassment as the glider's owners inspected their aircraft and prepared to carry it back. "I'm so sorry," she called to them. "I only just lifted it to see how light it was. I thought it was a kite."

"Don't tell me you've never seen a hang glider before?" one of the boys asked scornfully. "Where are you from?"

"Don't yell at her," Randy said, slipping an arm

around Chrissy's shoulders. "She comes from Iowa."

"Oh, well that explains it," the boys said, laughing. "They still drive around in covered wagons back there, don't they?"

There was good-natured laughter all around. Everybody seemed to think that the incident was very funny and a good story to tell around school next week. Only Caroline didn't join in the teasing, but she didn't look too pleased to see Chrissy, either.

Now I've gone and made a complete fool of myself again, Chrissy thought angrily. *I've just got to win that speech contest now or they'll all remember me as the biggest klutz ever!*

Chapter 5

"Chrissy?" Caroline pushed open the bedroom door that evening and looked at her cousin curiously. Chrissy was lying on the bed, staring at the ceiling. "Are you sick or something?" Caroline asked.

"No. I'm fine."

"Well then, are you coming?"

"Coming where?"

"Don't you remember? We decided that we'd all go and see that new comedy movie, *Horror High*? I told Tracy we'd pick her up at seven."

"You go ahead," Chrissy said. "I don't feel like coming tonight."

Caroline picked up her brush from the dresser and ran it through her blond hair. "You're not still waiting for Bart to call, are you?" she asked.

"What if I am?"

"Chrissy, if he were going to ask you out tonight, he'd have called before now. Now hurry up and get ready."

"He might still call," Chrissy said, not moving. "He's not the type of guy who likes to plan ahead."

"I think you're wasting your evening," Caroline remarked, pulling her hair back in neat combs. "It's supposed to be a good movie. Besides, it would do him good to find you out if he calls. He seems to like the idea that you sit around waiting for him to call."

"I happen to need him right now," Chrissy said. "I don't want to blow my chances of a date for the senior ball."

"Suit yourself," Caroline replied. "I'd better get going. I don't want to be late."

Chrissy heard the door shut as she lay there on the bed gazing at the rosy glow of evening light reflected from the building opposite.

Why hasn't Bart called this week? she wondered. She went through every detail of their last meeting—an eighteenth birthday party given for a classmate of Bart's at Forsythe, the exclusive private school he attended. It had been a fun evening, or so Chrissy had thought. And Bart had seemed to enjoy her company, if the ride home had been any indication. They had certainly parked outside long enough! When she'd finally gotten out of the car, he'd said his usual "See ya, Chrissy." He never tied down the "see ya" to where or when, but he always called, just before she got around to despairing.

She propped herself up on one elbow and glared at the phone. "Ring!" she commanded. "Ring right now."

Silence.

She frowned at it even harder, willing it to ring with all her powers. "I'm going to count to ten," she said, "and by the time I finish, he'll ring." She counted slowly and reached ten. "Maybe I should count to twenty," she said, and continued, but the only sound was the clanging of a cable car as it descended toward the Bay. "Not that sort of ring," Chrissy muttered.

She got up and began to pace, like a caged animal. *If he doesn't call in half an hour, I'll call him,* she thought. *And if his mother answers, well, I'll just put on my snobbiest voice and pretend I'm someone else. I've got to tell him about the ball. If I wait any longer it may be too late. . . .* Worrying thoughts began to creep into her mind. *What if it already is too late? What if he met another girl that he likes better and that's why he hasn't called?* The thought sent a chill down Chrissy's spine. Bart was far from perfect, she knew that, but he was sweet and funny, and very, very special—and she didn't want to lose him.

She continued pacing. "I'll put a spell on the phone," she decided. She knelt in front of it, staring at it very hard. "Alacazam, alacazee, you are in my spell," she intoned in a deep voice. "You will obey my every word. When I snap my fingers, you will ring! One, two, three!"

She jumped so violently that she nearly fell over backward when she heard the shrill ring. Trembling, she picked up the receiver. "Hello?" she stammered.

"This is the Handy Dandy Carpet Cleaning Company calling to see when you last had your carpets professionally cleaned," the voice said brightly.

"Yesterday!" Chrissy fibbed and slammed down the receiver. *Why the heck did I do that?* she asked herself. *That poor woman is only doing her job. It's not her fault Bart hasn't called.*

"I know, I'll get a sandwich," she said. "The moment I leave the room, I bet it rings!" She walked to the kitchen and fixed herself a triple decker with all the trimmings. But the phone still did not ring, even by the time she had finished the sandwich.

"I know, I'll take a shower," she decided. "Phones always ring when you are in the shower."

She stretched the cord so that the phone reached just outside the bathroom door. Then she left the door open as she hopped in the shower. When she finished the shower the phone still had not rung and the floor was soaking wet. She slipped on her robe and took her time mopping up the water. Still no call.

Dejected, Chrissy leaned against the door-frame and stared down at the tiled floor. *Well, I guess Cara was right*, she thought. *Bart isn't going to call.* She glanced up and happened to catch a glimpse of her reflection in the mirror above the sink. Her face was pink from the sun, and her nose was already starting to peel. Although her long blond hair was damp from the shower, Chrissy could still detect several flyaway split ends. *No wonder he's probably found another girl, the way I look. Well, I'll show him!*

Quickly, before she could lose her resolve, she raided Caroline's beauty collection as well as her aunt's and spread the products out before her. First she combed a conditioning pack through her hair, leaving it on to soak in. Then she smeared on an oatmeal face mask, letting it harden to a white crust while she painted her nails bright red. By the time she was through, she was feeling much more cheerful.

She put the finishing touches to her nails and was carefully screwing the top back onto the polish bottle when she heard a car pull up outside. She peered out the window to see a white convertible parking in front of the big Victorian apartment house.

"Holy cow!" Chrissy yelled. "It's Bart!"

For a moment she was rooted to the spot with horror.

"It's Bart. What am I going to do now? I'll hide. I'll pretend there's nobody home. No, I want to see him. Don't panic—think this through logically. It will take him a couple of minutes to climb the stairs, right? I can wash this stuff off my face and hair."

Then she acted, dashing like a madwoman into the bathroom, still telling herself not to panic as she turned the taps on full force to fill the sink. She didn't even have time to wait for the hot tap to heat up. Plunging her whole head into the basin, she had to stifle a yell as her head met very cold water! She clenched her teeth and scrubbed and splashed like crazy to remove both mask and conditioner. With water cascading from her head, she reached out to the towel rail, but the towel wasn't there. "Oh no," she wailed, realizing that she had left her towel in the bedroom. "Don't panic," she muttered again, as she staggered down the hall, trying to see through the curtain of dripping hair to find her way to the laundry closet. She grabbed the nearest towel and scrubbed savagely at her face. When she looked in the mirror this time, her face was even pinker than before and her hair was sticking up in all directions like a hay stack.

"Ahhggh!" she moaned again. She was just tearing a comb through her hair when the doorbell rang. Ignoring the chaos in the bathroom—the white streaks of mask clinging to the basin, towel and floor, the water slopped everywhere, and the telltale line of drips all the way down the hall—she tightened her robe around her and walked to the front door.

"Hi, Chrissy," Bart greeted her.

She draped herself casually against the doorpost. "Why, Bart. What a surprise," she cooed.

"I hope you don't mind my dropping by like

this," he said, doubt clouding his chiseled features. "I know I should have called earlier, but . . . anyway, I was out for a drive and I thought I'd just see if you were free. Were you doing anything special?"

"Me? No, just lying around, doing nothing much."

A smile lit up Bart's face. "Want to go out for Chinese food? I'm starving!"

"Sounds great, Bart. Come on in. It will only take me a minute to get ready."

She rushed in to the bedroom and slipped on her denim skirt and soft pink sweatshirt, quickly pulled her hair back in one of Caroline's hairbands, and tried to look cool, calm and collected as she returned to Bart in the living room.

Half an hour later they were sitting together in a booth in a cozy Chinese restaurant. It was one of the famous old-style restaurants where each table is in its own private room created by large decorative screens. Chrissy relaxed. She felt better than she had all week. She was sitting opposite Bart and he was smiling at her, that wonderful, crooked smile that made her melt inside.

"I just love places like this," she remarked. "It makes me feel like a real VIP to have a whole room in a restaurant." She leaned over to whisper to Bart. "Maybe the waiter thinks we're movie stars or important politicians or something!"

Bart shook his head, smiling into her eyes.

"You're quite a girl, Chrissy," he said. "I'm going to miss you when you're gone."

"You'll be too busy being Mr. Successful at Stanford," Chrissy teased, but her face was serious.

Bart shrugged. "Sometimes it doesn't seem real, does it?" he asked. "High school coming to an end, I mean. I'm not at all sure I want to leave. I've griped about it for four years but at least I feel comfortable at school. I know where the rest rooms are and where the cafeteria is . . ."

Chrissy started to giggle. "No, don't laugh," Bart went on. "Those things are important. I like to know my way around places. Have you seen how large the Stanford campus is? I might be lost for weeks there."

Chrissy looked at him with new insight. "You? I don't think you have much to worry about. You're the type of guy who can handle anything."

"Are you kidding? My mom had to hold my hand on the way to school for a whole month when I started first grade," he said, grinning at her. "I'd kind of like someone to hold my hand for the first month of college, too, but I have a vague suspicion that someone might tease me."

"I wouldn't mind holding your hand," Chrissy offered. "That would give me a good excuse to stay on in California. I'd phone home and say I can't come. I'm a professional hand-holder."

Bart's eyes grew serious. "You really want to stay here?" he asked.

Chrissy gave a big sigh. "I don't know," she said. "I miss my folks and the animals, and I even miss my brothers, but there's so much I'm going to miss here when I go back to Iowa. I've been here for two whole years of my life. I feel like a Californian now. I know I'll never be able to fit in again back there."

"You don't have to stay in Iowa," Bart said. "You can always do college and then move again."

"I know," Chrissy said, "But I'm like you. I get scared when I think about the future. I'd like things to go on like this forever—frozen in a senior year with my friends around me. . . ."

"What about all the good graduation things that are coming up?" Bart asked. "You'd never get those if you were frozen in your senior year."

"Oh, speaking of graduation things," Chrissy said, making her voice light even though her throat felt tight. "I didn't ask you yet about my senior ball. The tickets go on sale this week and I was hoping you'd come with me."

His eyes creased into a smile. "Of course I'll come with you. I'd love to. When is it?"

"May twenty-third," Chrissy answered calmly, but inside she was glowing. With Bart as her date, the senior ball would be perfect!

"I'll be there," he said. "How come it's so early? Ours isn't until June."

"They always have it over Memorial Day weekend," Chrissy said. She looked at Bart's face. "What's the matter?"

"Memorial Day?" he stammered. "Gee, I'm sorry, Chrissy. That's the weekend of our class trip. We're going to Hawaii."

"Hawaii?" Chrissy echoed.

Bart nodded. "Yeah. Forsythe always has its graduation trip there."

"Oh." For a moment Chrissy was speechless.

"I'm sorry," Bart said again. He was quiet for a moment. "I suppose it's a good thing you found out in time. Now you can ask someone else if you want."

"I guess so," Chrissy said hesitantly. She picked at a Chinese noodle with her chopsticks. Suddenly the food did not taste so appetizing. The noodle slid down like wet string. Her mind raced through all the things she had said to her friends about Bart, how she had boasted about bringing him to the ball, how she had looked forward to sweeping up those steps on his arm, noticing the envious glances of all the other girls.

"I suppose you're really set on going to Hawaii?" she asked in a small voice.

Bart avoided her gaze. "Well, to tell you the truth, I have been looking forward to it." He reached across the table to take her hand. "If it was any other weekend, Chrissy . . . Anyway, you'll probably have a better time with a guy from your crowd at school. You wouldn't want an outsider tagging along at your senior ball."

Chrissy knew that Bart was trying to make her feel better, but it wasn't working. In fact, she felt worse. She didn't want to go to the ball with anyone else.

Bart gave her hand a little squeeze. "Chrissy," he asked in a low voice. "Do you mind if I ask you a question?"

Chrissy's heart did a giant leap. *He really does feel bad about not coming with me to the ball*, she thought. *Maybe he's going to suggest a way he can make up for it. He's going to ask me something special and serious, I can tell by his face. . . .*

"Chrissy?" Bart said again, "Is something wrong with you?"

"Wrong with me?" Her voice trembled. What was he getting at?

"I only asked," he went on, looking slightly embarrassed, "because I've been looking at you all evening and I noticed these scaly patches of white clinging to the roots of your hair. I just wondered what . . ."

Chrissy put her hand up to her head and then realized what she was touching. She tried to ignore the blush that was creeping into her cheeks. "Oh, that?" she said casually. "That's just the remains of my face mask. I didn't manage to get it all off, I guess. I'm not an expert at face masks."

Bart's face lit up with amusement. "A face mask?" he asked. "What did you want with a face mask?"

"To make myself look better, I guess," she said, her face still warm with embarrassment.

Bart started to laugh. "You are funny," he said.

"As if you need to do anything to look better. I like you just the way you are."

"You do?" she stammered. Somehow the evening was no longer such a disappointment. Bart liked her just the way she was! At least that was some consolation for not going to the ball with him.

Chapter 6

On Monday morning, the talk at school was all about the senior ball—new dresses and tuxedos, limos and restaurants. It seemed to Chrissy that everyone in the world was going except her.

"Are you coming down to the office with me at lunch to buy your tickets?" Tracy asked, running to catch up with Chrissy after first period. "I'm meeting Maria and Justine and we're all going together."

"Er . . . I think I'm busy at lunch," Chrissy stammered. "Something I have to catch up on in the physiology lab."

"Better not leave it till too late," Tracy said. "Or you might find the tickets are all sold out."

"Sold out? Don't they have enough for

everybody?" Chrissy asked, hope beginning to
dawn.

"The ballroom can only hold so many people,"
Tracy said, "I'm sure they put a limit on it. I'd
hate for you to miss out. Besides, I'm counting on
a dance with the fabulous Bart. George is such a
boring dancer. It'll take me half the night just to
get him on the dance floor."

They reached Chrissy's classroom door.

"Try and make it at lunch, okay?" Tracy asked
with a hopeful smile. "We'll save you a place in
line."

"I'll try," Chrissy lied. She walked to her seat
and mechanically spread her papers in front of
her. Why had she lied to Tracy? Why hadn't she
just come right out and told her that Bart wasn't
coming? Well, at least she now had a way to
escape. She could picture it now: *I'm sorry, guys,
but Bart and I won't be joining you . . . I was so
busy that all the tickets had gone by the time I got
to the office. But never mind, Bart has promised
to take me to a fantastic restaurant instead and
the next week we'll be going to his ball. . . .*

That brought her back to reality again with a
bump. He had been so sweet and nice on
Saturday and he'd seemed genuinely sorry about
not being able to join her. But he hadn't said,
"Don't worry, we'll go to my ball instead." He'd
mentioned that his senior ball was in June, but
why hadn't he invited her? Was he planning to
take a girl from his own school instead? Chrissy
felt hot and cold all over when she imagined

another girl dancing in Bart's arms. *I really like him a lot*, she thought. *But, it's certainly obvious that I like him a lot more than he likes me.*

When lunch came around Chrissy deliberately slipped out through the back door of the gym and made her way up the hill behind the school to the park where she and her friends usually ate lunch. As Chrissy had expected, the park was deserted. She was glad that the others were busy buying their tickets so she could be alone. She had walked up the hill at a fast pace and now stood at the entrance to the park, feeling her heart pounding from the climb and her cheeks tingling in the brisk wind. Up here it felt as if she were on top of the world. She could watch cable cars inching their way down the steep hills like ponderous black beetles and people scurrying around down at Fisherman's Wharf like tiny ants. The yachts on the Bay, looked like toy boats in a giant bathtub and beyond the water, the hills, still green from the winter rains, folded over one another like pleats in a skirt.

Chrissy walked to the nearest bench and sat down. Why did life have to be so complicated? As soon as she'd sorted out one mess, it seemed as if another one sprang up to take its place. *The only thing left now is the speech*, she thought. *That's the one important thing left before I leave. . . .*

She stared out across the Bay, her mind as blank as ever when it came to topics. She had leafed through old volumes of the school newspaper and found that the speeches had all been

only one step away from Nobel prizes, as Justine
had said. Chrissy shuddered. How could she com-
pete with "Creative Solutions for the Garbage
Crisis," "Does Nuclear Power Have a Place in Our
Future?" and "Earthquake Prediction: Are We
Any Nearer to Preventing Disaster When the Big
One Strikes?"

If only Caroline would be a little more helpful.
More than once Chrissy had nudged her about
coming up with an idea and each time Caroline
had acted as if she hadn't heard. *I just don't get it,*
Chrissy mused. *It seems like Cara isn't even trying
to help.*

Suddenly Chrissy drew a sharp breath as a
shadow fell across her. She had been so deep in
thought that she hadn't noticed anyone else enter
the park.

"Oh, Chrissy, it is you," a deep voice said. "I
thought that looked like your hair, streaming out
in the breeze."

Chrissy looked up to see a tall, serious young
man smiling down at her, blinking in the strong
light through wire-rimmed glasses, his dark hair
falling, as always, across his forehead, looking
ridiculously like a young Clark Kent about to turn
into Superman.

"Alex!" Chrissy said in delight.

Alex Bauman had been Caroline's boyfriend
when Chrissy had first arrived in California two
years ago. He and Chrissy had quickly become
good friends. In fact, at one time Caroline had
been suspicious of their relationship, although

Chrissy had assured her that they were just friends. But since he and Caroline had broken up Alex seemed to spend all of his time with his new girlfriend, a bouncy redhead named Jan.

"You don't know how you scared me, coming up behind me like that," she said, giving him a big smile. "What are you doing up here anyway?" she asked.

"I was about to ask you the same question," he said. "Mind if I sit down or did you come up here to be alone?"

"I came up here to escape buying tickets for the ball," she confessed. Somehow she found it so easy to talk to Alex. When she'd been terribly homesick during her first few difficult months, she'd confided in Alex. And now she found herself telling him about her disappointment over Bart.

When she had finished, he nodded, as if he understood. "So you don't want to go at all without him?" he asked.

"Are you kidding?" Chrissy asked. "Of course I want to go. It's just the question of somebody to go with. All the boys left without dates are . . . well, let's put it this way—if the Martians landed on Earth and were greeted by these guys, they wouldn't get a clear idea of what humans looked like!"

Alex threw back his head and laughed. "Not as bad as that, surely," he said. "I think you're a little too tough on us guys."

"Us guys?" Chrissy said. "Come on, Alex. I'm

talking about guys like Brian Bennet, who has the worst crush on Cara right now. You have to admit he's an arch geek if there ever was one. I'm not talking about you—just the guys who don't have dates for the ball."

"But I'm in that category right now," Alex said. "I am, like you, totally dateless. . . ."

"But you and Jan?" Chrissy stammered.

"Are no more," Alex finished, dropping his eyes as he spoke to watch his sneaker draw patterns on the sandy path.

"You broke up with Jan?"

"Not exactly. She broke up with me," he said, attempting a smile. "It seems that Bob Burger asked her to go to the ball with him and she just couldn't turn down the captain of the football team."

"Boy, what a jerk!" Chrissy exclaimed. "You two were going together for a long time, weren't you?"

Alex nodded. "A year and a half. But I guess it was bound to happen sooner or later. We were different people, you know. I was busy applying to colleges and she was forever complaining that I didn't spend enough time with her. You know how it is."

"I remember," Chrissy said. "You went through the same thing with Caroline, when she didn't have any time to spend with you."

Alex's cheeks flushed. "I guess I did. How is Cara these days? I hardly see her around school. We don't have any of the same classes."

"She's fine."

"Still going with the guy she met in Iowa?" he asked casually.

"Going with him? They're practically engaged!" Chrissy said with a laugh. "She writes to him, he writes to her. She phones him, he phones her. They're trying to go to the same college. . . ."

Alex shook his head. "I can't imagine Caroline falling for a guy from a farm. She's such a city kind of person. You know what I mean, don't you?"

"You mean we're all backward, uncultured louts who talk about nothing but pigs and corn, and whose idea of a good time is to sit on the porch, chewing on hay, right?"

"Of course I don't . . ."

"That's okay Alex. In some ways you're right," Chrissy said. "But Luke isn't like that at all. I think he'll be a writer someday. He and Cara are great for each other."

"I see," Alex nodded. "I'm glad for her. She seems to have her future all sewn up. . . ." He drew a diamond in the sand with his toe. "So that leaves you and me without a date for the ball, right?" he said.

"Are you thinking what I'm thinking, Alex?" Chrissy asked excitedly. "We could go together— just as friends, I mean. We'd split the costs, half and half. . . ."

"You mean I'm better than the other geeks,

nerds, and weirdos who are available?" he asked with a grin.

"Are you kidding? You'd be a perfect escort, Alex. We'll have a great time," Chrissy said. "That is, if you want to go to the ball with me."

"You bet I do," he replied, his brown eyes twinkling in anticipation. "Come on, let's run down to the office and get those tickets right now."

He took her hand and together they flew down the hill.

Chapter 7

Dear Luke,

Another bombshell has just dropped. Chrissy burst in, all excited, yelling that she was going to the senior ball with Alex! You remember I told you about Alex—I used to go out with him before I met you.

I heard a rumor over the weekend that he'd broken up with Jan and it suddenly occurred to me that I could ask him to go to the ball with me. Don't worry. There's no reason for you to get jealous. He's just a nice guy, but I don't feel anything for him anymore except as friends. That's why he would have been a good date for the ball—we could relax and have fun together without anyone getting the wrong idea. But I guess that Chrissy got in first, as usual. She always seems to have a knack of getting in first with everything. Sometimes I wonder if she wasn't put into my life just to spite me, because everything I try to do, she does it quicker and better!

When she broke this news to me—yelling all the way up from the street, you can imagine—I wanted to tell her that I'd been considering asking Alex myself and that she might have consulted with me first. But once again, she was so full of herself and so loud and bouncy, that I just couldn't find the words. She just barges right ahead as if she is the only person who matters in life!

Now it looks like I'll be the only person from my group who doesn't go to the senior ball ... unless I go with dear Brian Bennet, and I'm not thrilled about that prospect. Brian is one of the biggest nerds at Maxwell, and everyone says he has a crush on me. Yuck! I've seen him trying to sneak up on me several times and I've managed to run and hide. Today I had to spend fifteen minutes of my lunch hour in the girls' bathroom because he was waiting outside. I knew he was still there, luckily, because he was talking to one of his creepy friends, and I could hear them both laughing—one like a hyena and the other like a chicken! Boy, would I have a wild time with them at the ball.

Oh, Luke, if only San Francisco was a little closer to Iowa. I suppose there's no chance of you flying over here in your crop-dusting plane for the ball? No, I didn't think so. There's not much chance of me jetting to Danbury for your prom, either. Sorry. I hope you find someone to go with.

Incidentally, Chrissy had the nerve, after dropping the Alex bombshell, to ask how I was
coming along with ideas for her speech! Wait
until she finds out that I've also signed up for it,
and I've come up with a great idea, too! After all,
I started the campaign to save the park last year
and I worked really hard to save those old houses
the year before, so I decided to talk on preserva-
tion versus progress in the modern city. Let's see
Chrissy's face when she finds out!

I've just read this through and I sound like a
real meanie, don't I? But I can't help it. For two
whole years I've had to put Chrissy first. It's like
I haven't mattered at all, and for once in my life
I want to matter. I don't want to drift out of high
school as if I'd never existed.

Well, that's enough complaining for one letter.
As usual, Luke, thanks for listening. You're the
greatest!

Love, Cara

From the moment she had the silver and blue
tickets in her hand, Chrissy couldn't stop thinking
about the ball. She spent the first three periods of
the following day dreaming about dresses and
hairstyles. Since the colors for the ball were
silver and blue, Chrissy thought that she and
Alex might dress to match. She visualized herself
in a floating silver dress that sparkled as she
walked, with a light blue corsage on her wrist
and blue flowers in her hair. And Alex would
look great in a gray tux with a blue cummerbund.

Wait until she told Bart about that! Maybe he'd finally feel jealous and wish that he wasn't going to Hawaii after all. Should she phone him up to tell him? *Oh Bart, I thought I'd just let you know that I've found a partner for the ball, so I wouldn't want you to worry about me. Yes, he's an old friend actually, and he looks a little like Christopher Reeve. . . .*

No—that might not be the wisest thing to do. Instead of getting jealous, he might decide that their relationship wasn't worth fighting for.

Why is it so hard to know what boys are thinking? Chrissy wondered as she headed down the hall to her fourth-period class. Especially Bart—he's like Dr. Jekyll and Mr. Hyde, she mused, pausing in front of the main office to check the notice board. There was the old notice about the sale of the tickets, and one scholarship still open for honors Latin students, and . . . Chrissy stood there with her mouth open as she stared at the last notice.

SENIOR SPEECH
PRELIMINARY CONTEST THURSDAY, MAY 21
AUDITORIUM

Because only two seniors have signed up so far, we have extended the sign-up deadline. How about it, seniors? This is your chance to make your voice heard at graduation. More seniors are encouraged to try out for this prestigious contest.

Already signed: C. Madden. C. Kirby.

For once in her life, Chrissy was speechless.
She continued to stare at it, open mouthed,
unable even to breathe. She even blinked a few
times, as if she might be having a hallucination
and a blink might make it go away. But each time
she opened her eyes, the name C. Kirby leaped
back at her from the wall.

It's some mistake, she told herself. *There is a
perfectly reasonable explanation for this. They
knew Caroline was helping me with my speech so
they put her name down, too, as a kind of campaign manager . . . or maybe it's not Caroline at
all. There must be more than one C. Kirby in a big
school like this. I bet it's a Christopher Kirby I've
never met and he's going to be talking on something boring like the international monetary
system and he'll be no threat to me at all. . . .*

But her little pep talk did not do much to calm
the nagging fear that clenched her stomach.

I'll settle this once and for all, Chrissy decided.
*I'll go find Cara right now. She knows how much
I wanted this speech. She wouldn't dream of running against me and spoiling my chances. I'm
sure of it. . . .*

She was still muttering to herself as she pushed
through the crowd of students and made her way
toward the physics lab where she knew Caroline
had her next class. Sure enough, Caroline was
just coming down the hall from the opposite
direction. Her hair was loose, draped prettily
around her shoulders and glistening like pure
gold where the sun fell on it through the win-

dows. She was talking to a tall, earnest-looking boy, nodding politely as if she was trying hard to get interested in what he was saying. She looked exactly how Chrissy always thought of her cousin—sweet, gentle, and too considerate to ever hurt anyone's feelings. . . .

There must be some mistake, she said to herself again.

She stepped forward, blocking Caroline's path.

"Cara?"

"Oh, hi, Chrissy" Caroline said. "Is something wrong?"

"That's what I was about to ask you," Chrissy said, noting Caroline's eyes looking at her uneasily. "I've just seen a notice on the board about the speech contest. Your name is down there, right next to mine. That's a mistake, right?"

"Why should it be a mistake?" Caroline asked evenly.

"You mean it's not a mistake? You mean you're entering the contest?"

"Right," Caroline answered, still calm even though her cheeks were very pink.

"Cara—how could you?" Chrissy exploded.

"It's open to all seniors, Chrissy," Caroline said, taking a step back from her cousin. "Why shouldn't I want to enter it, too?"

"You knew I wanted it, that's why!" Chrissy yelled. "You knew how badly I wanted to do something special before I left here. You knew I was really looking forward to it and counting on it and you entered just to spite me! I can't believe you'd do a thing like that!"

Chrissy was yelling so loudly that students were turning to look all the way down the hall. Caroline's cheeks were flaming now, but she still sounded calm when she spoke.

"Did it ever occur to you, Chrissy, that I might want it, too?"

"Why should you want it? You've done lots of things," Chrissy stormed.

"But I haven't gotten much credit for anything," Caroline replied, her own voice rising now. "I mean, I did all the organizing to save the park and you stole a damn bulldozer and got all the publicity! I coached you in ballet for the school musical and you got the solo! Maybe it's my turn to do something now!"

"But not the thing I wanted to do! That's not fair! You pretended like you were going to help me and all the time you were going behind my back!"

"Wrong!" Caroline snapped. "You took it for granted I was going to help you! You wanted me to do all the work again and let you get all the credit as usual. Well, it's about time you learned that people are not going to give in to you all your life, Chrissy Madden. You can't always play poor little helpless me and expect people to fall for it!"

"I do not act like that!"

"You do, too! . . ." Caroline's voice rose an octave as she tried to imitate Chrissy's puppy-dog face. "Oh, Cara, I need to try out for the musical and I'm scared to go alone!"

"Maybe you're jealous because I've managed to do a few things better than you! You were kind to me when I was your poor little helpless cousin from the boonies, but now that I'm a threat, you can't take it."

"I can take it very well," Caroline said. "It sounds like you're the one who can't take it. If you think you're just as good, then you shouldn't mind competing against me for the speech. You write your speech, I'll write mine. Whoever wins, wins fair and square." Caroline looked up at the last students disappearing into the lab. "Now, if you'll excuse me, I'm going to be late for class."

"But, Cara!" Chrissy called after her. "You can't do this to me. I don't stand a chance against someone smart like you! Cara!!!"

But when Caroline did not turn back, Chrissy stomped off down the hall in disgust. Now on top of everything, she was late for class.

Chapter 8

"Where's Cara?" Tracy asked, glancing back into the school building as she and Chrissy walked down the steps. "Shouldn't we wait for her?"

"I expect she's still in the library," Chrissy said shortly, "working on her famous speech!"

Tracy turned and looked at Chrissy steadily. "Chrissy, did you and Caroline have a fight?" she asked. "When Caroline came into physics she looked as if she was about to burst into tears any minute, and when I mentioned you, she said she was staying out of your way until you cooled down."

"Until I cooled down?" Chrissy echoed, her cheeks turning pink. "She made it sound as if I did all the fighting as usual, while she was little Miss Cool and Reasonable!"

"She did say you were being totally unreasonable right now," Tracy said with a wry smile. "You're not mad because she entered the speech contest, are you?"

"Wouldn't you be mad," Chrissy snapped, "if you'd set your heart on one last thing to bring you fame and fortune before you left California forever, and you asked your cousin to help you with it, and instead she went behind your back and entered the contest herself?"

"But you didn't think you'd be the only person in the contest, did you?" Tracy asked. "Why shouldn't Cara enter if she wants to? Wouldn't you rather your cousin beat you than a total stranger if you had to lose?"

"No!" Chrissy exclaimed. "I'd rather not lose at all, and Cara just makes one extra contestant to spread the votes around." She paused as they reached a traffic light and slapped her hand against the CROSS NOW button. "She knew how much I wanted this, Tracy. I told her a million times."

Tracy looked uncomfortable. "I don't want to get in the middle of this," she said. "You are both my friends. I don't like to see you falling out— especially not right before you go home. All I can say is that I know Caroline very well. If she's entered this, she must want it very badly. She usually hates getting up in front of an audience."

"So she should let me do it instead," Chrissy insisted. "I don't mind facing an audience at all. I want everyone to remember me!"

"Maybe she'd like everyone to remember her, too," Tracy suggested calmly. "It is her school, too, you know. She's worked very hard at Maxwell for a lot of years, but she's never been in the limelight. And she's missed out on all the school scholarships so far, although I'm sure she deserved one. Maybe she'd like to shine for once!"

"I guess so," Chrissy said uneasily, remembering all the evenings Caroline had come home late after working on this committee or that. She was always up long after Chrissy, still working on her homework and Chrissy knew how disappointed Caroline was at not receiving a scholarship. "But why does she have to shine at the same time as me?" she wondered aloud.

Tracy laughed. "There's not much left to shine at, is there? All we have left is a trip to Disneyland, a senior ball, and a week of finals before graduation. She can hardly shine on the Matterhorn or Space Mountain, can she, and she says she's not coming to the senior ball. . . ."

"She's not?" Chrissy asked uneasily.

"She can't think of anyone to go with. She told me she would have asked Alex but you got in first."

"Oh," Chrissy said, feeling embarrassment creeping up her cheeks again. It had never occurred to her that Caroline would want to ask Alex, but it made sense. *Cara could have had a good time at the ball with Alex*, Chrissy thought. *They're still friends, but the romance between them was over ages ago, so Cara wouldn't have needed to worry about being disloyal to Luke. Alex would have been the perfect date for her.*

Chrissy and Tracy climbed up the hill together, both silent as they put all their effort into walking up the steep incline. Uncomfortable thoughts were beginning to buzz around inside Chrissy's head. Had she been thinking only of herself too much? Had Caroline counted on going to the ball with Alex and been too shy to say so?

They reached the corner and stood panting as a cable car clanged past with tourists clinging to the sides.

"I've got to go, Chrissy," Tracy said. "I have to baby-sit at four and I need a snack first. They're into health food at the house where I baby-sit and all they leave out to snack on is these disgusting bran bars." She started to walk away from Chrissy, then, quickly looked back. "I'd talk it out with Cara if I were you," she added. "You don't want to spoil two good years together by a fight at this stage!"

Chrissy waved to Tracy and walked on. There was a stiff breeze blowing up from the bay today. Wisps of mist still clung around the towers of the Golden Gate Bridge and further out in the ocean a solid bank of fog was threatening to move in and swallow up the city. Chrissy shivered. San Francisco would be perfect in the summertime if it weren't for the fog. It always seemed to come in and spoil lovely summer days—in much the same way as unexpected complications always seemed to spoil her plans.

Why did Cara have to enter the speech contest? I really don't want to end my stay here with a fight, she thought. *Families can stay apart for years over one silly fight. I mean, look what happened in Mom's family.* A cold blast of wind fanned her warm cheeks as she recalled her mother telling her about the argument. It seemed so silly now, but years ago Aunt Edith and Grandma and Grandpa Hansen had been at loggerheads. As a result, Chrissy hadn't even known until two years ago that she had a cousin in San Francisco. *I can't let that happen again,* she vowed.

She really did want to do the speech, but she had to admit that she would probably survive without it. *There will be other speeches and other things I can do,* she thought. *Besides, Caroline is smarter than me. She probably will give a better speech.* Chrissy thought about her topic. She had decided to talk on the plight of the American farmer and the future of agriculture. As she went through the points in her head they seemed trite and wishy-washy. Perhaps nobody in California would be interested in farmers anyway. Most of them thought that milk came from a milk factory! *And yet it seems to be the only thing I know enough about,* she thought. *Should I step down and let Caroline win the speech contest?*

She headed slowly down the last stretch of the hill, batting arguments back and forth in her

mind like ping-pong balls. A picture popped into
her head of Caroline's face looking proud and
happy at the end of her dance recital long ago.
Caroline had given up ballet now. Although
Chrissy knew she didn't regret quitting, she also
knew that Caroline missed the satisfaction of
knowing she did something especially well.

But I've never had anything that I do especially
well, Chrissy reflected. Another picture popped
into her mind of Stefan, the gymnastics coach,
telling her that she could be a great star if she
worked hard. But she hadn't had the guts or
determination to go through with it, and Caroline
had been the only one who understood that she'd
rather be out having fun.

She's such a nice person, Chrissy thought. *And
she works so hard for what she wants. Not like
me*, said a small voice in her head. *Maybe she
deserves the speech more than I do.*

She began to climb the steep steps from the
street to the Kirby's third floor apartment in the
old Victorian-style house. Chrissy looked up with
contentment at the curly wood carvings around
the porch and tower that were known as ginger-
bread trim. She had enjoyed living here, and she
didn't want to spoil her special memories. She
stomped up the last steps and paused to get her
breath outside the front door. *Out of shape*, she
said to herself. *Once I'm back on the farm I'll
need to get back in shape again pretty quick or I
won't be any use to anybody. . . .*

She opened the door with her key and dropped

her backpack in the front hall. She had expected to be in the house alone this afternoon, but to her surprise, she heard voices coming from the bedroom she shared with Caroline. So Caroline had not stayed in the library. She had hurried home ahead of Chrissy— *obviously trying to avoid me*, Chrissy thought uncomfortably. She was about to open the bedroom door when she realized that Caroline did not have a visitor—she was talking on the phone. Hastily Chrissy backed away from the door again and was about to turn and get herself a snack when she heard her name mentioned.

". . . and she made a big scene, right there in the school hallway," Caroline was saying. "I could have died, Maria. She was yelling at me and everyone was staring!"

Chrissy shifted uneasily from foot to foot, commanding herself to go to the kitchen, but unable to move.

"I can't see why she's getting so upset," Caroline went on. "I mean, she didn't honestly think she'd stand a chance of winning the speech contest, did she?" She giggled. "What on earth do you think she can talk about? I mean, I don't think a speech on 'How I Raised Pigs' is going to do it, do you?"

Chrissy felt herself getting hotter and hotter. She kept telling herself not to listen, but she still could not move away.

"Yes, I know she's really set her heart on it," Caroline went on, "but I did try to tell her. She'll have to see that only a really brilliant speech is going to win! I don't even know how much chance I've got, but it's sure to be better than hers."

Another pause.

"You know what I think, Maria—I really think that she believes she'll charm the audience with her down-home personality, just like she did when she got that solo in the school musical! But what she doesn't realize was that she only got the solo because she is a natural-born hillbilly! It won't get her a speech on graduation day."

Another pause. "Oh, Maria, why are you defending her? She always wants her own way." Caroline burst into laughter. "I've got it! Remember how she wanted a live piglet to dance with in the musical? Well, we should give her one to use as a prop for her speech! That could be cute—we'd put a little cap and gown on him!!!"

Chrissy could feel anger building up inside her head like steam in a kettle. How dare Cara make fun of her behind her back!

". . . yes, Maria. I think I'll just have to have a little talk with her, suggest she step down before she makes a fool of herself!"

The steam inside Chrissy's head exploded. She flung open the bedroom door and stood, glaring at the surprised Caroline. "If you think I'm stepping down to make way for you, you are wrong, buster!" she yelled.

"Why, Chrissy, I'd no idea you were home," Caroline stammered.

"That was perfectly obvious. You wouldn't be brave enough to make fun of me to my face. If I can wrestle a hog to the ground, then it wouldn't take much effort to squash a creepy little worm like you!"

"Chrissy—calm down a minute," Caroline said, her face growing hot with embarrassment. "What you say when you're joking with friends . . . you don't really mean it. We were just having fun . . . being silly, you know?"

"Oh sure, fun at my expense. And don't tell me you didn't really mean that I should step down in favor of you, so that you could get all the glory without any competition!"

Caroline toyed with the phone in her hand, looking at it nervously. "It wasn't that, Chrissy. I don't want you to step down so that I can win. If I win, I want to win fairly. It was you I was thinking of . . . you're not really the type. I didn't want you to be embarrassed. . . ."

Chrissy's cheeks were now radish red and her eyes glinted dangerously. "Oh sure. I bet you were thinking of me—the same way you were thinking of me when you dared me to ski down that expert slope my second day on skis. Well, you should know by now—I'm not a quitter, and I don't scare so easy. I wouldn't give up this contest now if I had to speak against my own mother! I'll be glad to speak against you, but I will not be speaking *to* you, Caroline Kirby. You want war, and you've got it. From now on we are enemies!"

Chapter 9

"There's someone at the door for you," Caroline told Chrissy in a harsh voice, her face flushing pink. Only a moment ago Chrissy had announced that she never wanted to speak to her cousin again.

Chrissy was lying on her bed, attempting to read all twelve hundred pages of *Don Quixote* for English class in one sitting. She felt no better than her cousin. Her mind was a maze of anger and guilt and she had read the same page at least five times without understanding it. There seemed little hope for finishing the rest of the book.

"Who is it?" she asked, as if talking to a stranger. She staggered to her feet.

Caroline shrugged her shoulders and walked

out of the room to the kitchen. With a frustrated sigh, Chrissy went to the living room.

"Bart?" she said in surprise, realizing as she stood there that she was in her oldest sweats, with holes in both knees, that her hair was like a giant mop, and that she had probably smudged her eye makeup.

"Hi, Chrissy," he said, rising from the sofa and smiling as if he was delighted to see her.

"But it's not Saturday," Chrissy stammered. "I didn't expect to see you."

The smile broadened. "You know me," he said. "I hate to be a creature of habit. There's a new movie that starts tonight that's supposed to be really good. I thought you might want to go with me."

Chrissy thought of her tousled appearance, *Don Quixote* lying unread on her bed and then weighed them up against the chance of spending an extra evening with Bart. Without a doubt, Bart won. "I'll just go change," she said, running her fingers through the tangles.

Bart sat back into the sofa. "No problem," he said. "No hurry."

Chrissy flew into the bedroom. For once she'd have to make do with her own clothes and makeup. There would be no more borrowing of Cara's nice outfits or Cara's special blusher. She opted for a long white sundress, looked longingly at Caroline's white clogs and then stuffed her feet into her own, slightly shabby canvas pumps. A savage brush through her hair, a quick ponytail and retouching of her mascara and she bounded out again, transformed into the usual image of cheerful, bouncy Chrissy.

"Not bad," Bart commented, slipping an arm around her shoulder while he drew her toward him and planted a little kiss on her cheek. "That must hold the world's record for quick transformation."

Chrissy thought back to the last time he had arrived unannounced and her transformation from face mask to human being. This was nothing compared to that!

"So, how are your graduation plans coming along?" he asked. "We just had a meeting on the Hawaii trip today. Sounds really great. We have a hotel right on the beach. So far we've planned a barbeque on the beach, a day trip to Diamond Head, and a big luau for the last night. I heard that last year someone arranged for real hula dancers to come to the luau and give everyone lessons . . ." Bart chatted on happily, laughing at his own descriptions, while Chrissy sat quietly beside him.

She'd been so pleased to see him, but now each word about Hawaii made her feel more and more resentful. Of course he was looking forward to this trip—that was understandable—but did he have to rub in the fact that he'd be missing her senior ball? *Maybe he's already forgotten*, Chrissy thought sadly.

His descriptions and plans for Hawaii lasted all the way to the movie theater. Chrissy had done no more than make polite noises of interest and said, "That's great," until she sounded like a parrot.

Then, as they turned into the parking lot, he suddenly seemed to notice her again. "Find yourself a date for your ball yet?" he asked casually.

"Yes, I did, as a matter of fact," she said. "I'm going with a guy named Alex. He's a really nice guy—great looking and smart, too. And he was the star of the soccer team."

"Sounds boring," Bart cut in with a grin.

"Not at all," Chrissy said, trying to give a knowing look of satisfaction. "In fact he's fun to be around. Good sense of humor, you know, and he's the sort of guy you can talk to. I've always liked him, but he's been going with this girl called Jan for a whole year."

She had hoped that her glowing description of Alex would stir up a little jealousy in Bart. She glanced at him for signs of worry in his face, but he was as relaxed as ever.

"I can't understand that," he said.

"Understand what?"

"Getting yourself tied down to one girl for a whole year. I know kids who've been going with one person for four whole years of high school and they plan to get married the moment they graduate. Can you believe that? What a waste of a life!"

"If they've found the right person, I guess it's okay," Chrissy said thoughtfully. Only two years ago, she'd been intending to do just that with Ben

Hatcher back in Danbury. She was glad now that she had a different future ahead of her, but that didn't mean it was the wrong choice for everyone.

"Think about it, Chrissy!" Bart said forcefully. "How can they possibly know they are right for each other? I bet those marriages always end in divorce, just like my parents."

Chrissy looked at Bart in surprise. "I didn't know your parents were divorced," she said quietly.

"They will be soon," Bart said with a short laugh. "After arguing politely for twenty years, my dad has finally moved out and now their lawyers are doing the fighting instead."

"Oh, Bart, I'm sorry," Chrissy said.

Bart looked away from her. "Don't be," he said. "I'm used to it. It's nothing new to me. I guess I've seen it coming for years. I suppose it wasn't much of a marriage—both out doing their own thing, traveling in different directions, but it does make a guy feel insecure when the separation is finally legal. It's like you don't exist anymore."

Chrissy didn't know what to say. How could she help him feel better? At last she reached out to touch him but he moved away.

"Hey, don't go feeling sorry for me," he said. "I don't want anybody to feel sorry for me. I'm having a great life. Who needs parents? I'm almost an adult anyway—but I'll tell you one thing. I don't plan to mess up my life the way they have. I'm going to stay cool and hang loose."

He looked across at her and laughed at her puzzled expression. "Hey, come on, Chrissy. Loosen up. Don't go serious on me. You know me—I don't plan to take anything seriously until I turn thirty. Cool, unattached and unencumbered. My parents' big mistake was to get married right out of high school, and look how that turned out. . . ."

"Not all early marriages turn out bad," Chrissy said. "My folks got married right out of high school, too, and they're very happy. But I agree with you—I wouldn't want that sort of life. There's too much to do and see."

Bart turned to her and reached across to squeeze her hand. "We really understand each other, Chrissy," he said. "That's why I'm real glad you didn't make a big thing of your senior ball. You were real cool about that and I'm glad you've got another date." He paused and inhaled deeply. "What am I saying? I'm sorry, Chrissy. I'm not making much sense tonight. I really would have liked to go to the ball with you. I like you a lot, Chrissy, but it's good we're not getting too serious. Let's just have fun, okay?"

He smiled encouragingly. "I'm sure you'll have a great time at your ball with what's-his-name, and I plan to have a blast in Hawaii! That's the way life should be lived."

Chrissy swallowed hard. "You don't have to worry about me," she said lightly. "I can always take care of myself pretty well."

"You're a great girl, Chrissy," Bart said. "Thanks for not pressuring me."

"That's me," Chrissy said, climbing out of the car. "Nonpressure Chrissy!"

She managed to keep a bright smile on her face until they were in the darkness of the movie theater.

"What is this movie?" she asked. "I don't think I've heard of it before."

"That's because it's Russian," Bart said. "Subtitled, of course. But it got great reviews. It's about two concert pianists, one Russian and one American, and they meet at an international competition."

The movie began, and Chrissy relaxed onto Bart's shoulder, hoping to lose her worries in the fantasy on the screen. As the story progressed, however, she realized that she would rather have watched any other movie in the world than this one! She could have handled aliens turning people into cabbages, or cops and robbers chasing each other, or even maniacs running amok in high schools. But she found that a tragic love story only succeeded in making her feel worse. She could barely watch as the Russian pianist on the screen got caught trying to defect to be with his American girl friend. And a lump formed in her throat when the pianist was sent to Siberia, where he got frostbite which ruined his hands.

"I gave it all up for you, Elizabeth," he told the American girl. "But it was worth it—no sacrifice is too great for one you love. I have your music to sing to me now. What I have given up does not matter. . . ."

Usually Chrissy and her friends would have giggled at a corny scene like that, but Chrissy had already had enough emotional upheavals in one day to last a lifetime. Suddenly a great hiccoughing sob escaped from her. Tears began to stream down her cheeks. Vladimir was willing to give up his fingers for the one he loved. Elizabeth was so lucky to have a man like that.

Bart turned to her. "What's wrong?"

"Nothing," she sobbed, trying to stifle the crying and dry her eyes with a tissue.

"Are you sure you're okay?" he whispered.

She tried to answer, but another sob came out. The credits began to roll on the screen and the lights came on. Bart got to his feet, looking down at her in concern.

"Why are you crying?" he asked softly.

"Because nothing like that will ever happen to me," she gasped between sobs.

"You want to lose your fingers to frostbite?" he teased, but his voice was suddenly harsh. He took her arm and pulled her firmly to her feet. "Come on, Chrissy. Cut it out . . . it wasn't that sad."

Chrissy nodded, but tears continued to pour down her cheeks. People were beginning to file past them, staring suspiciously at Chrissy. Bart grabbed at her hand. "Let's get out of here. People are staring. You're embarrassing me."

"I can't help it," she stammered, stumbling

after him as he tried to push past the crowd and make a quick exit. "It was so sad."

"I thought it was pretty corny, actually," he said. "Really overdone. I wouldn't have bothered if I'd known. And it got such good reviews, too."

By the time they got to the car Chrissy had her sobs under control, but still they drove straight home, without stopping for the usual cappuccino or ice cream. Bart drove faster than usual and when they screeched to a halt, he didn't put his arm around her to kiss her good night. Instead he sat silently in the driver's seat, staring straight ahead. Chrissy could hear her heart pounding as she waited for Bart to speak.

"I guess I've been a real jerk tonight," Bart said at last.

Chrissy looked at him, but he continued to avoid her eyes. "That's okay," she replied softly. "I didn't exactly help the situation." She kissed him gently on the cheek. "I'll be here if you ever need me, Bart." Then without looking back she climbed out of the car.

Silently she let herself into the apartment. If only she and Caroline were still friends. She really needed someone to talk to right now, but there was no way that she was going to give in.

Caroline and her mother were seated in the kitchen, drinking a late-night cup of tea together.

"Ah, Chrissy dear," her aunt called. "Like a little nightcap?"

"Er, no, thank you," Chrissy said, turning her

face away from the light so that nobody saw her red eyes. "I have a ton of stuff to do."

"So are you girls all packed for Disneyland?" Caroline's mother asked cheerfully.

"We're not sleeping there, Mom," Caroline said. She sounded cheerful and normal, as if nothing unusual had gone on today.

Caroline's mother rolled her eyes in horror. "You're going to spend all night on those rides?" she asked.

"That's the fun of it," Caroline said. "The whole of Disneyland just for us and about five thousand other high school seniors . . . and there are famous rock bands playing all night. I only hope I can keep going that long. I'm scared I'll fall asleep on a bench and the bus will leave without me!"

Caroline's mother laughed. "Oh, I'm sure Chrissy wouldn't let them go without you. She'll keep you going all night, if I know Chrissy. Remember when we took you to Disneyland last year? We were all ready to drop and Chrissy was still begging us to go on the Matterhorn one more time—right Chrissy?"

"I . . . guess so," Chrissy said. She looked at Caroline. "I think I'll go pack . . ."

"But I thought you didn't need to bring anything," her aunt said, with an amused glance.

"Then I'll go pack the things I don't need," she said, walking hurriedly past the kitchen.

She gave a big sigh as she closed the bedroom door behind her. It was very tiring to try and keep her fight with Caroline from her aunt and

uncle. She was still determined not to talk to
Caroline again, but she didn't want to upset
Caroline's parents. It was not easy to pretend that
she and Cara were getting along just fine. She
had to eat twice as much at meals so that she
never had time for conversation and she had to
act extra busy around the house, too.

I'm tired, Chrissy thought. *I wanted to enjoy my
last weeks of school but it seems like everything's
going wrong! I've quarreled with my cousin and
now I've even blown it with Bart!*

Chrissy shuddered at the memory of it and her
eyes threatened to fill with tears again. Really,
she was becoming such a crybaby! Back home
she hardly ever cried. She usually prided herself
on being tough, so what was the matter with her
now?

*You knew that you'd be leaving Bart soon
anyway,* she told herself. *Only a few more weeks
and you'll be back in good old Iowa and you'll
never see him again, so you'd better get used to it!*

She began to pace the bedroom, but instead of
clearing her mind all she could think was no Bart,
no Caroline, no speech!

*Maybe it would be better if I just packed my
things and took off for Iowa right now,* she
thought. *There sure isn't much to look forward to
here anymore.*

*What, and arrive just in time to watch Tammy
Laudenschlager make the graduation speech
back there?* she answered herself. *No way!
Besides, I don't want to miss out on Disneyland. I*

only hope I can stay well clear of Caroline so she doesn't spoil that night for me, too!

She paused by Caroline's desk. Right on top was a letter that Caroline had started to Luke. Chrissy glanced down at the paper. Her own name jumped out at her in several places.

"Chrissy is being such a pain right now," Caroline had written. "You know how much I wanted to enjoy my last weeks of high school with my friends, but Chrissy has spoiled all that. She's making me feel that I have to creep around in my own house, avoiding a scene with her. I wish I could smooth things over again, but the only way to do that would be to back down and let Chrissy win the speech with my help—and I'm tired of always backing down for her. Luke, I'm just so furious. Graduation time is supposed to be so special, but thanks to Chrissy it's horrible. And the worst thing is that she doesn't seem to care a bit!"

Chrissy turned away from the page, a sob threatening to come up in her throat again. Maybe some of that was true, and yet Caroline had only written her side. She hadn't written how she made fun of her cousin and thought of her as a great big zero! She hadn't written that she had spoiled Chrissy's chances of making the speech and had ruined graduation for Chrissy.

Chrissy flung herself down onto her bed with a sigh, then yelped as she collided with the corner of *Don Quixote*, still lying on the pillow. She picked it up and flung it onto the floor. Who cared about Don Quixote? It didn't even seem to matter if she flunked English right now. Nothing seemed to matter any more. She turned to look at the picture of her family that she kept on the dresser: her dad in his usual checked shirt, squinting his eyes against the light, her mom embarrassed as always when she had her picture taken, but the gentle kindness in her face showing through.

I wish I was with you right now, she thought. *It's been too long since anyone hugged me, and that's just what I need right now—a great big hug!*

Chapter 10

The bus rolled through never-changing California countryside—rolling hills still green from winter rains, dotted with purple lupins and bright orange poppies. They seemed to have been driving forever, passing only clusters of gas stations and fast-food restaurants, suspended in a time warp between San Francisco and Los Angeles.

"I wish I could sleep," Chrissy said, "because I know I'm going to need all my energy to get the most out of tonight."

Tracy, in the seat beside her, only grunted.

"Are you asleep, Tracy?" Chrissy asked, giving her a gentle prod. Tracy's eyes opened slowly to focus on Chrissy. "I was," she said.

"Lucky you—I can never sleep on buses."

"I could, if the person beside me did not keep bouncing around and yelling in my ear," Tracy said. "I wish you and Caroline had not had this dumb fight so that you could sit together. She can never sleep on these long drives either."

Chrissy glanced across the aisle to where Caroline was sitting beside a girl they hardly knew. She felt a pang of guilt as she saw Caroline's head turned toward the window. She had made Caroline odd man out by claiming Tracy as a partner, knowing that Tracy was too softhearted to say no. Chrissy knew she hadn't been fair—after all, Tracy had been Caroline's friend first. *Well, that's too bad*, Chrissy decided resolutely, as Maria turned around from the seat in front.

"Here, would you guys like some cookies?" she asked. "Baked fresh this morning."

"Gee, thanks," Chrissy said, taking a cookie. "I didn't realize how hungry I was. It's hours since we stopped for lunch."

"It is not, Chrissy. It's only an hour at the most," Tracy said with a weary smile. "I can never understand how you don't look like a blimp."

"I burn it all off with my nervous energy," Chrissy said.

"Pass the cookies over to Caroline," Maria instructed.

Chrissy dropped the cookies onto Tracy's lap as if they were still hot. "Would you ask that girl over there if she wants a cookie?" she said.

Before Tracy could answer, Caroline looked

up. "Would you please tell that girl beside you that I don't want a cookie, thank you very much."

"Would you tell that girl that she's missing out on something really good!" Chrissy answered back. "It's chocolate chip. Her favorite."

"Would you remind her that eating on a bus always makes me carsick," Caroline said smoothly.

"You mean bus-sick," Chrissy countered. "I mean, would you tell her she means bus-sick."

"And would you tell her that I know perfectly well what I mean and I don't need her to tell me," Caroline said, turning away to the window again.

Chrissy finished the cookie she was holding. It was still gooey and crammed with chocolate chips and pieces of nuts, but somehow it did not taste so good any more.

"I wish you guys would stop this craziness," Tracy said. "It's wearing us out to be in the middle. I like you both, Chrissy. I don't want to have to take sides."

"Nobody's asking you to take sides," Chrissy answered.

"Yes you are—by asking me to sit beside you, I've had to choose not to sit beside Cara, so now she thinks I'm against her, which isn't true," Tracy explained. "Surely you can forget your differences and enjoy the trip, can't you? A graduation trip will only happen once in your lifetimes."

"She has to apologize to me first," Chrissy said firmly. "She was the one who signed up for the speech competition behind my back and then made fun of me to everyone. I've done nothing to her. If she wants to say she's sorry and that she's getting out of the contest, that's just fine with me."

"Fat chance," Caroline said, turning briefly from the window.

Tracy sighed. "I get the feeling it's going to be a long night," she murmured.

The sun was just setting as the bus dropped down from the hills in the sprawling Los Angeles basin, basking in its usual smoggy haze. Those who had been drowsing woke up and the bus began to buzz with excited conversation.

"I don't know why everyone's making such a big deal about Disneyland," Chrissy heard a voice behind her say. "I mean, Disneyland's a little kid's place really. I don't know why we bothered to come. It's going to be so boring."

"I've already been a million times," her companion answered. "I've only come to listen to the rock groups."

Normally Chrissy would have been shouting and bouncing around in anticipation. She had to admit that she was excited about seeing Disneyland again, but as a result of her quarrel with Caroline, she was a bit more subdued than usual. *Well, I have one thing to be grateful to Cara for*, she thought, staring out of the window at the rows of streets and palm trees now flashing past. *At least she prevented me from making a fool of myself.*

She half-listened to the conversations going on all around her about the number of times everyone had been to Disneyland and how everyone wished the class trip had been to Hawaii or somewhere exciting instead. She let herself dream about being in Hawaii with Bart before she remembered that she probably wouldn't be seeing him again. He had only called her once since the embarrassing incident at the movie theater, and then the call had only been to say that he was going to be busy all weekend and he hoped she enjoyed Disneyland. The sort of distant, polite way he spoke to her made her think that he was trying to find a way to tell her that everything was over. So much for trying to be an understanding girlfriend.

I hope someone will come on the rides with me, she thought suddenly. If everyone else was so bored, would they want to go on all the rides Chrissy had enjoyed on her last visit to Disneyland? Chrissy hated to do things alone. There was no fun in doing anything unless you could grab somebody else and scream together. Would her friends understand that she had only spent one day in Disneyland in her entire life and that she wanted to do every single ride again? She imagined herself sneaking around in Fantasyland, waiting until nobody from her school was near before she leaped onto Mr. Toad's Wild Ride or Dumbo's Flying Elephants. *If only Cara . . .* she thought, remembering the good time they'd had together here last year, how they had laughed at the dumbest kiddie rides and screamed on the scary ones.

She glanced across at her cousin. Caroline was staring straight ahead, as if she was making a strong effort not to look in Chrissy's direction. Chrissy nudged Tracy. "You will come on some rides with me, won't you?" she asked. "I hate to ride alone."

"Er . . . sure," Tracy said. "But I expect we'll all go around in a big group anyway."

The bus turned into the Disneyland parking lot and the kids climbed down stiffly after so many hours of not moving. The air was warm and slightly scented, reminding them that they had come a long way south. The other buses from Maxwell soon joined them and their chaperon gave a speech about the reputation of the school and fitting behavior before he led them to the main gate. "And remember," he issued one last warning. "The bus leaves in the morning at seven sharp. Anyone not here will have to walk home." Weak laughter.

The students of Maxwell High began to move like an invading army toward the main gate. As they neared the entrance, all those kids who had talked about being bored on the bus, now began to sound a lot like Chrissy. "I'm going on the Matterhorn first!" a boy yelled.

"First?"

"Yeah—you chicken?"

"Space Mountain's better than the Matterhorn."

"No way. Space Mountain's lame."

"I have to get my photo taken with Winnie the Pooh this time!"

"I've got to get one of those Mickey Mouse hats with my name on it. I lost the last one."

"That will look cute at Harvard next year!"

Laughing, shouting, teasing, they surged forward through the special gate that was open for them. Chrissy found herself swept along, her heart pounding excitedly. Inside, Main Street was already crowded with seniors from other high schools. Senior Night seemed to be a popular event at Disneyland. The air was throbbing with the beat of a distant rock band and students were running eagerly from one activity to the next, not wanting to waste a moment.

"Let's get on Pirates of the Caribbean before everyone else does," Maria yelled in Chrissy's ear. They hurried down the remainder of Main Street, past the lake, where the paddle steamer was just making its rounds, and joined the line for the Pirates ride.

"I can't believe the short line," Tracy exclaimed delightedly as they moved straight into the building and were soon sitting on a boat, all piled in together. Caroline was sitting on the far side of the seat, as if she wanted to be as far away from Chrissy as possible. The boat began to move forward into the darkness. They teetered for a moment, then shot down the first waterfall, where a great spray of water splashed into their boat. Chrissy got some in her face, but Caroline got drenched.

"I'm soaked," she complained. "I got it all over me."

"The person on that end always does," Maria said soothingly. "Never mind, it's warm outside. It will soon dry."

Chrissy smiled to herself in the darkness, then felt mean for smiling. Why did she always have to feel so guilty about being angry with Cara? After what Cara had done, she deserved to be more than soaked!

She struggled with her feelings throughout the rest of the ride, giving sideways glances at Caroline as she attempted to dry herself off with tissues. Chrissy couldn't help recalling the other time they had ridden The Pirates of the Caribbean. They had laughed at the noisy pirate models and clutched each other in half-fright when a cannon ball exploded beside them. The last time it had been pure magic and fantasy, but now the edge had been taken off. Chrissy was aware that the pirates were not real and that the cannon ball was only a sound effect and a splash. The ride came to an end and they walked on, combing the water out of their hair, to the Haunted Mansion. Chrissy remembered how scared she had been moving backward into the darkness in a hooded coffin-seat. Thank goodness Cara had been beside her.

"Ride with me, Tracy," Chrissy heard Caroline

ask as they began to descend in the haunted room to the level below.

Quickly Chrissy slipped her arm through Tracy's. "She already promised to go on the rides with me, didn't you, Tracy?" she said, glaring at Caroline.

"Chrissy, I said we'd all ride together," Tracy said firmly, looking from one to the other.

"But only two can fit in these cars," Chrissy insisted, pulling Tracy into line with her. Luckily their turn came before Tracy could object.

I'm glad that wasn't me, she thought. *I'd hate to be on this ride alone—to have a ghost come in the car with me and nobody to grab.* And again she felt guilty that Cara was now having to face it alone.

When they got off the car she was gone.

"Where can Caroline be?" Tracy asked, looking around.

"Probably with Justine and Randy," Maria said, clutching at her boyfriend Dino as if he was about to run away. "Come on, Dino—you promised to go on It's a Small World, just for me."

Dino looked embarrassed. "The guys will tease me," he grunted.

"No they won't. Look, isn't that Brett from the football team standing in line ahead?" she asked, giggling.

They went on more rides, danced, ate, then did it all again. They did not bump into Caroline or Justine all night. They met Alex on Startours around midnight and he said he'd just ridden

Space Mountain with Caroline. They met Brian
Bennet around four in the morning, just coming
out of the Country Bear Jamboree, and he asked
them where Caroline was. By six Chrissy's feet
felt as if they were going to fall off at any
moment.

"I don't think we've sat down all night," she
complained to Tracy. "I'd love to dip my toes in
that lake right now."

"I don't think they'd let you," Tracy said.
"Come on. We still haven't got our free photo
with Donald Duck."

By the time the photo was taken, they barely
had time to browse through the shops on Main
Street before heading for the bus.

"I can't imagine where twelve hours went,"
Maria said, shaking her head.

"I know where it went. It went on It's a Small
World," Dino growled.

"Come on, admit you liked it," Maria said,
smiling fondly at him. "You thought those little
Hawaiian girls were cute!"

"Hmmph," Dino said. "That was just to shut
you up."

"Stop being a grouch and let's buy some
souvenirs," Maria said, dragging him toward a
gift shop. "I'd like something special for me and
I promised to take home some Mickey Mouse
ears for my little brothers."

Chrissy had bought some ears for her own little
brothers last year, so this time she got a pretty
china dog who looked a lot like their own Bonnie

for her parents and some candy for her aunt and uncle.

It was only when they got back to the bus that they discovered Caroline was missing. Justine and Randy had been with her until about midnight, but nobody had seen her after that.

"She said she wanted to take a rest and listen to a concert," Justine said. "We told her we'd be over at Startours but we didn't see her again after that."

Their chaperon looked angrily at his watch. "Someone must know where this girl is," he snapped. "Is she the sort who would play a stupid prank like this?"

"Not at all," Justine said.

"Something must have happened to her," Maria agreed.

"Who are her friends? Didn't she go around with anybody?" the chaperon demanded.

"She was with us to start with," Tracy said, "but we lost her."

Chrissy was beginning to feel worse and worse. She vividly remembered grabbing Tracy's arm and saying that Tracy was riding with her in the Haunted Mansion. There was only one reason that Caroline had not been with her friends, and she was that reason.

"We'd better alert park security and put out messages over loudspeakers," the chaperon said. "And some of you better go look for her. We pay for these buses by the hour, you know."

Chrissy ran with Caroline's other friends back

down Main Street. They hardly spoke and their faces were tight-lipped and worried. Nothing bad could happen to a person in Disneyland, could it? Disneyland was supposed to be a safe, happy place. So where could she be?

As she began to search through the park, endless terrible possibilities flashed through Chrissy's head. What was there to stop a crazy person from sticking a gun in her back and kidnapping her right out of the park? If something did happen, it would be all her fault. Every ride suddenly seemed to have dark corners behind it. . . ."

"We've got to find her," Chrissy insisted to one of the security men.

"Don't worry, young lady. Maybe she just fell asleep on a bench somewhere. People get tired, you know," he said soothingly.

"Not Cara. She would have woken up."

"Then she's locked in a rest room or got on the wrong bus!"

"That's it—the wrong bus!" Chrissy sprinted back to the bus depot again, but none of the buses had an extra student on board. All the buses except theirs were revving up, preparing to leave. Their occupants were staring anxiously out of windows.

Chrissy felt dangerously near to crying. She imagined watching missing-girl bulletins on television, seeing Caroline's face on the side of milk cartons and grocery bags, her aunt and uncle silent and scared . . . *If only we hadn't had the silly fight*, she thought. *As if a silly speech matters* . . .

Back in the amusement park, the search party had doubled, with several of the Disney characters joining the security patrol. The whole scene had taken on the quality of a black comedy. *If I weren't so scared, I'd think this was funny*, Chrissy thought, as she searched the rest rooms along Main Street with Donald Duck and two of Snow White's dwarves.

Holy mazoly, someone tell me that I've fallen asleep and this is just a bad dream.

Suddenly she heard her name being called. "Chrissy—it's all right. We've found her!"

Maria and Tracy were running toward her jubilantly. "We've found her. She's okay!" they shouted.

"The dumbest thing!" Tracy yelled, laughing with relief. "She went on Peter Pan's ride to get away from Brian Bennet. As usual, he'd been chasing her all night. Anyway, the ride broke down, right when she was flying over London. It was pitch dark in there and she was all alone, up in the air!"

"She was the only person on the ride and it seems that they forgot she was on it," Maria added excitedly, "so they took their time fixing the ride and she was up there for a whole hour before anyone heard her yelling!"

"Poor old Cara—can you imagine. What a shock. Thank heavens it wasn't the Haunted Mansion. Imagine being stuck in the Haunted

Mansion alone for an hour. I'd have died of fright. The maintenance men took her back to their little shack and gave her a cup of tea, but she's fine now."

"Come on—the bus is waiting for you!" Maria said. She grabbed Chrissy's arm and dragged her toward the bus.

Thoughts were flying around inside Chrissy's head. Number one was an enormous sense of relief. But when she saw Caroline standing beside the bus surrounded by a bunch of other kids, she felt a twinge of jealousy. *Well, Cara sure does go to a lot of trouble to get noticed*, she thought bitterly. *This must be part of her campaign to win the speech contest.* Caroline looked up as Tracy, Maria and Chrissy arrived.

"Here's Chrissy. She was searching the rest rooms with Donald Duck and a couple of dwarves," Maria said, and there was loud laughter.

"Finally. We can go," the chaperon said, looking at Chrissy as if the whole delay had suddenly become her fault.

Caroline looked up shyly at Chrissy. "I hear you were looking for me?" she asked.

"Only because they wouldn't let us leave without you," Chrissy said and climbed onto the bus ahead of her.

Chapter 11

Saturday, May 16

Dear Luke,

We got back from Disneyland early this morning, and I've just woken up from a nap. Chrissy is still snoring in the bed, but I couldn't really sleep. I'm still pretty shaken up by the big scare I had at Disneyland. The whole evening turned out to be a disaster—and you know how much I was looking forward to it. First of all Chrissy still wasn't speaking to me on the bus, which made it very embarrassing. Then, the first thing that happened to me in Disneyland was that I got soaked on the Pirates of the Caribbean ride. The others thought it was funny, but I was really soaked and it didn't feel funny at all.

Then, the very next ride, Chrissy grabbed

Tracy to be her partner all evening and I never saw them again. I had to ride most of the rides by myself. I wish you'd been there. Someday, we'll have to go to Disneyland together. Anyway, Randy and Justine came around with me for some of the time, but most of the rides are for two and I didn't want to butt in, so I always rode alone. I even lost them in the middle of the night.

The only person I couldn't lose was BB!!! (The geeky guy who has a crush on me.) I can't even write his name, he makes me so mad. I've told him about you a million times, but it obviously hasn't gotten through his thick head. Last night I even told him that I prefer to ride alone, but he still wouldn't take the hint. Everything I lined up for, he was right there behind me, grinning like an ape. I had to spend half the night dodging into ladies' bathrooms. Then, when I was trapped in the middle of Fantasyland, I saw him coming toward me. He hadn't seen me, luckily, and I jumped onto the nearest ride. It turned out to be Peter Pan, and a big mistake. I had just flown out over London in my ship when there was a grinding noise, and then all the lights went out. I didn't dare move because I was right up in the air. I yelled, but nobody came. It took hours before I was rescued. it kind of reminded me of the time you and I got stranded in that blizzard, remember? But this time I didn't have a cute guy to cheer me up!

Anyway, after sitting there, terrified that everyone would leave without me, a security guard finally found me. Everyone made a big fuss over me except Chrissy, of course. It seemed like she hardly noticed I was missing. I bet she would secretly have been glad if I'd never shown up. Some cousin I'm stuck with.

Well, I hope you found a date for your prom. I can't help being a little jealous, only because I wish your date was me. But I want you to go and have a good time. I think I've decided I'm going to ask James to the ball. He's on the Senior Gift Committee with me. We're just friends—he's got a mad crush on another girl, so don't worry. You're the only guy for me.

Love, Cara

"The problem of farming in today's economy is that it is not productive to farm small areas. . . ." Chrissy scribbled in her government notebook. Far away across the room her government teacher's voice droned on, boring as always, talking about amendments to the Constitution. Miss Peters was a nice enough person, just very boring. She opened her mouth every day and facts spouted out. She expected her students to make notes of these facts, but she didn't give many tests, and she never looked at homework. She also never seemed to notice if her students were doing something else while she talked, so Chrissy usually took the opportunity to catch up on her math for her trig class which followed.

Since she had started working seriously on her speech, however, she spent the period writing about farms. She was determined that her speech was going to be better than Caroline's, no matter what. Caroline's speech would be smart and meaningful, but Chrissy was sure that if she could only come up with a good topic and some good facts, she could put them across better than Caroline. Today was the deadline for sign-ups in the speech contest and when Chrissy had last checked the board, nobody else had signed up. So all Chrissy had to do was to beat her cousin! That shouldn't be too hard—maybe she could even psych Caroline out by talking casually about the large crowd and how awful it would be if she lost her notes or got a frog in her throat. . . . *I'm becoming a mean and horrible person*, she thought. *I will not resort to low tricks like psyching somebody out. If I win, I want to win fairly!*

She glanced down at what she had scribbled on the paper. She had been searching for the perfect opening sentence and still could not come up with the right one. This one was too cold. An opening sentence had to appeal to the emotions of the audience! She crossed it out and began again:

"Imagine that you are a farmer in the midwest. Your family has had this plot of land for a hundred years and now you are being evicted because you can't repay your debts. . . ."

No! That sounds too corny, she decided. *I wish I could think of something funny to start with. Good jokes always win an audience, but it's hard to make jokes about something as serious as this!*

"A funny thing happened to me on the way to losing my family farm," she wrote, then scribbled over it with deep, dark strokes. Her own family had almost lost their farm and it hurt too much to joke about. At that moment the bell sounded and the rest of the class fought to reach the exit first, leaving Miss Peters in mid-amendment. Chrissy gathered up her things and followed the stampede. She had almost reached the door when Miss Peters called her over.

"Oh, Chrissy, could I have a word with you, please?"

Chrissy turned back to join her teacher. Since Miss Peters was also one of the teachers in charge of the speech contest, she figured the conversation would be about that.

"Yes, Miss Peters?" she replied.

"How is your speech coming along?" Miss Peters asked, still smiling pleasantly.

"Fine, thank you," Chrissy answered. She wondered for a moment if Miss Peters was not as blind as everyone thought. Did she know what Chrissy had been doing for the past hour?

"I hope you'll be able to attend the graduation ceremony, if you win the contest," Miss Peters said quietly.

"Oh sure I will," Chrissy said, smiling easily. "I wouldn't plan to leave before my graduation, you know. This will be a really big day for me. I just wish my folks could fly over to see me. . . ." She looked at Miss Peters's face. It was kind but serious. "What do you mean you hope I'll be able to attend?" asked, her voice wavering.

"Chrissy," Miss Peters began, "I really want you to graduate with the rest of your class but . . ."

"But?" Chrissy stammered.

"You are about to fail government, Chrissy," her teacher said softly.

"Fail government?" Chrissy shrieked. "Nobody fails government!"

Miss Peters gave a little smile, then quickly turned serious again. "They do if they don't pay attention in class and they get below a passing grade on the one test I've given all semester." She looked at Chrissy, her forehead creased in a worried frown. "Government is a serious class, Chrissy. It is not a Mickey Mouse course. It is not a homework period. I don't think you've answered one question I've asked this semester."

Chrissy's face flushed red. "I have trig next and I'm always struggling with that," she said. "And everyone always said that . . ." her voice trailed off.

Miss Peters picked up for her, "That government didn't matter?" she finished, shaking her head. "You will not be the only person in for a shock today," she said. "There are quite a few other students who will be hearing from me that they are in danger of not graduating at all."

"So what do I have to do?" Chrissy asked. "Or is it too late? I'm not doomed already, am I?"

Miss Peters smiled. "No, you're not doomed

already. I don't check homework because I expect seniors to be responsible enough to study on their own. You can bring me your homework notebook, all up to date, and get a passing grade on the final if you want to graduate."

"My homework notebook?" Chrissy stammered again.

"If you've done the homework it should be no problem, Chrissy," Miss Peters said. "Now you'd better hurry if you don't want to be late for your next class . . . oh, and Chrissy—keep working on your speech!"

Chrissy ran out into the hallway, her heart still beating very fast. This was all a bad dream! She had to graduate! Surely they couldn't not let you graduate because you failed one dumb class, could they? She shivered suddenly as if she had stepped into a draft. Imagine not even graduating! She pictured phoning her parents to tell them the terrible news, watching Caroline trying not to look smug, and her friends whispering behind her back at school. She pictured sitting at the back of the darkened auditorium, watching Caroline and everyone else walk up onto the stage and come down with diplomas and everyone hugging and kissing afterward, leaving her to slink away alone. . . . There was no way she could not graduate now. She had to get together a homework notebook and pass that crummy final. If she really studied hard, she could probably scrape through the final, but the homework notebook was a big problem. She'd hardly done any of the homework—somehow, other things had always seemed more urgent. *I bet Caroline has all her homework notes in perfect order*, she thought. *If only Caroline and I were still . . .*

She drifted along the hallway, hardly noticing where she was headed, until she recognized Brian Bennet's spiky blond hair and thick-rimmed glasses up ahead. He seemed to be staring at the notice board. *He's probably gazing at Caroline's name*, Chrissy couldn't help thinking with a smile, *or thinking of ways to get rid of me so that his beloved can win the contest!*

She couldn't resist pausing by the notice board to see her own name on the sign-up sheet. After a quick glance, Chrissy continued down the hall. But she had only taken two steps when she was drawn back in horror for a second look at the sign-up sheet. Sure enough, another name had been added to the list.

"Brian Bennet?" Chrissy yelled in disbelief.

He turned around at the sound of his name and a big grin spread across his face. "Oh, hi there, Chrissy," he said sheepishly. "I guess you're rather surprised to find me entered in the contest, right?"

"Right," Chrissy managed to say. She had to bite her tongue to prevent herself from saying that she would have been less surprised to find one of the gorillas from the San Francisco Zoo entered, or even a passing Martian!

"Me, too," Brian said. "But now that I've gotten

over the shock, I'm sort of getting excited about it."

Chrissy stared at him as if he had switched to speaking Chinese. "You mean you didn't enter this contest yourself?" she asked.

"Heck, no," he replied. "I wouldn't have had the nerve. But I guess other people thought I'd be the right sort of person. I got a letter through my locker this morning urging me to enter. At first I didn't pay any attention, but obviously someone must have thought I had a good chance if they entered me as a write-in candidate."

"Someone entered you as a write-in?" Chrissy could hardly make her tongue and lips form the words.

"Better than a write-off, eh?" And he broke into his hyena laugh, making Chrissy cringe with embarrassment.

"That's what they told me," Brian said. "Pretty darn nice of them, don't you think?"

"Oh sure," Chrissy said. "But who entered you? Did they tell you?"

"I've no idea," he said, still grinning happily. "It was an anonymous letter, but it sure makes a guy feel good to know that he is thought of as a great orator by his peers. I'm going to have to do some research work this weekend if I want to stand a chance against you guys. I guess you have your speeches all written, right?"

"Uh, right," Chrissy said.

"I thought as much," Brian answered. "I know it will be a tough challenge for me, especially against Caroline. You don't think she'll be mad at me, do you? I don't want this to ruin our relationship, but I could hardly disappoint my public, could I?"

"I guess not," Chrissy mumbled.

"I'll create a speech that will make her proud of me," Brian went on happily. "I am not without ideas, or without expertise in the field of microcomputers. Also several interesting topics have presented themselves to me in physics over the course of the year. May I ask what topic you have chosen for your speech, or is it a deep dark secret?"

"Top secret," Chrissy mumbled. She began to walk away.

"Good luck, rival speechmaker," he called after her, "and tell Caroline hi for me. Tell her I can't wait to be standing beside her on the stage. . . ."

Chrissy broke into a run as his voice wafted after her. *Brian Bennet in the speech contest! That was absurd. Who would want to listen to Brian Bennet talk about computers? Someone had played a cruel joke on him, that was all. Who would ever have nominated him? Anybody in their right mind would choose someone like Caroline over Brian . . .* a sudden thought made Chrissy shiver. *What if Caroline herself had nominated him to pay him back for making her life miserable? Or worse still, what if she had nominated him to take votes away from her cousin?* Chrissy could almost hear Caroline's voice after the contest. "Poor old Chrissy. She wasn't even good enough to beat a geek like Brian Bennet."

Chrissy shivered again. Why were such weird thoughts floating around in her head lately? *Surely Caroline wouldn't do such a horrible thing, would she? Yet she was now Chrissy's worst enemy, and enemies were capable of anything.* Chrissy's mind was still spinning as she slipped into the girl's bathroom before her next class. To her dismay, Caroline was already there, calmly drawing a brush through her silky blond hair. Chrissy had a sudden desire to grab Caroline and shake her.

"I suppose you've heard about the other candidate?" she blurted out, making Caroline spin around with her hairbrush poised in midair.

"Other candidate, for what?" she asked. Chrissy thought her voice sounded just a little too innocent.

"So you know nothing about it?" she asked sweetly. "It wasn't your idea?"

"What are you talking about?" Caroline demanded.

"You mean you didn't plan the whole thing to take votes away from me? It was pretty smart of you—choosing someone who couldn't possibly beat you, but who might take a few votes away from someone like me."

Caroline slowly lowered her hairbrush. "Chrissy—what are you talking about?" she demanded again.

"About your friend Brian Bennet," Chrissy said.

"What about him?"

"You mean you really don't know? He's now entered as a candidate in the speech contest against both of us," Chrissy announced.

"Brian Bennet? In the speech contest?" Caroline yelled. She lowered her voice in an effort to maintain her composure. "You're putting me on!"

Chrissy shook her head. "No way," she said. "I've just seen him. And I've seen the notice board, too."

"I'm surprised he would have the nerve to enter the speech contest," Caroline remarked, the surprise still evident in her voice.

"He didn't enter it. Someone entered for him, as a write-in candidate," Chrissy said, not taking her eyes off Caroline's face for a second. "I wondered if maybe you did?"

"Me?" Caroline shrieked. "Are you crazy? Listen, I'd like to stay as far away from Brian Bennet as possible. How do you think I could give my best speech with that stupid grin three inches away from me? I bet you entered him yourself, to psych me out and now you're just putting on this act to establish your innocence. It's just the kind of underhanded thing you would do."

"Thanks a lot," Chrissy yelled back. "If that's all you think of me, I guess I'd better be getting to math class. I'm already late."

"Yeah—you have to pass math if you want to graduate and make that speech," Caroline said with a grin.

"I hate you," Chrissy muttered. She turned and fled. What had Caroline meant by that comment about not graduating? Was it just a snide remark, or did she know what Miss Peters had said? *I've just got to graduate*, Chrissy told herself, but her stomach was tight with fear.

Chapter 12

By the time the school day came to an end, Chrissy felt ready to escape and hide in a big hole until graduation was safely over. She could not remember ever feeling worse, even when she'd thought she might lose Ben to Tammy Laudenschlager, even when she had fallen down a mountain skiing or turned into the human radish with poison oak at summer camp. Those were all temporary setbacks, even though they had each seemed like the end of the world at the time. But not graduating? That would mean no college in the fall, no speech contest, no senior ball, no nothing.

Chrissy swallowed hard to stop a sob that was lurking in the back of her throat. It looked as if the speech contest was off, anyway. All her spare time would have to be spent working on those homework assignments to make a notebook for government class and studying to pass the final. Now Caroline would win the speech contest without even trying and Chrissy would have to watch her cousin giving the speech, even if she did manage to make it to the graduation ceremony.

She pushed past milling students at the front entrance and ran down the steps. She just wanted to get away from everybody right now. She had a horrible feeling that if she bumped into Tracy or one of the others wanting to walk home with her, she would disgrace herself and start crying.

"Hey, Chrissy, wait up. What's your hurry?"

She jumped as someone grabbed her arm. She was swung around to face Alex smiling down at her as if today was just like any other day in the universe.

"Oh, Alex," she stammered. "It's you."

He laughed. "Well, don't look so startled. You look as if I was the ghost of Christmas past about to haunt you."

"Sorry," Chrissy said, managing a weak smile. "I was miles and miles away."

"Thinking about your famous speech?" he asked.

"Er, no, not exactly," she mumbled. "I was, I mean, I have things on my mind right now," she said unable to come up with any reasonable excuse for stumbling around like a zombie. She wasn't in the mood to talk to anyone—not even Alex.

"Oh, I see," Alex said, and Chrissy sensed that he realized his presence wasn't wanted. "I guess you're on your way somewhere special and you're in a hurry." He paused and looked at her as if he suspected she might be trying to escape from him. "I hope our date for the ball is still on," he added uncertainly.

"The ball? Oh sure, Alex," Chrissy stammered.

"That's good," he said brightly. "I'm sure looking forward to it, Chrissy. We'd better get together some time soon and make some serious plans—like where we're going for dinner and what we're going to wear. Have you chosen your dress yet?"

"Er, not yet," she said.

"Then you'd better get a move on if you don't want to be escorted by someone wearing a purple tux designed for a midget," Alex said. "All the good ones go if you don't order early . . ."

Normally Chrissy would have giggled at the thought of Alex in a purple tux designed for a midget, but today her mouth felt as if it was frozen into a grim line.

"You do still want to go with me, don't you?" Alex asked hesitantly. "I mean, if you've got someone you'd rather go with . . ."

"Oh no, Alex, of course I want to go with you," Chrissy said quickly. "You'll have to excuse me if I'm acting weird today. I've got a lot of things on my mind."

"You want to talk about them?" he asked. "Remember I'm a great listener."

"I remember, Alex," she said managing a faint copy of her normally dazzling smile. "I'll always be grateful for having you to talk to, but right now I don't feel like talking to anybody. There's nothing anyone can do for me right now. I have to sort some things out for myself."

"Sounds really tragic," Alex said. "All right, I can take a hint. I'm on my way . . . only please don't take too long choosing the dress. Imagine if I get a red cummerbund and you end up with bright green? We'll look like a Christmas tree."

Chrissy managed to giggle at that. "I promise I won't get a green dress, Alex," she said. "And I'll definitely go soon to look for a dress. Shopping always takes my mind off my troubles."

"Why don't you go shopping with Cara?" Alex asked. "I thought there was some rule that girls always had to go shopping in twos."

Chrissy looked away from him. "Caroline and I aren't getting along too well right now," she said.

Immediately his eyes were attentive again. "Oh?"

"Actually more than that," she said, "we're hardly speaking to each other."

"You had a fight?"

"You could say that. I was so excited about the speech contest and then she signed up behind my back and . . . oh, a whole lot of other stuff. It just built up, worse and worse. I guess we've been cooped up together for too long and we've both gotten on each other's nerves."

"I'm sorry to hear that," Alex said. "I bet Cara's feeling as bad as you are. She hates fights, I know that."

"You sound like you're on her side," Chrissy said.

"No . . . no, I'm not, Chrissy," Alex said. "It's just that I used to know Cara pretty well and I still . . . well, I don't like to see two friends of mine spoiling the last of their time together. Isn't there any way you can talk this over and make up?"

"I don't think so, Alex," Chrissy said. "Things have gone too far for that. We just get into another fight every time we talk. She wasn't even the least bit grateful that I'd rushed around like a crazy woman looking for her when she was lost at Disneyland. I guess she doesn't like me any more than I like her right now."

"I'm sorry," Alex said again. "I suppose I can't ask you to tell her hi from me?"

"I could do that much for you, Alex," Chrissy said with a small smile.

"Good," he said, with a grin. "And call me, Chrissy, when you've picked out your dress, okay?"

"I will, Alex," she said as he waved and jogged off in the other direction.

Alex is so nice, Chrissy thought. *I suppose I should have told him that I might not be able to go to the ball.* She gave a determined sigh. *I'm going to go to that ball, one way or another. In fact, I'm going to go shopping for that dress this very minute. A new dress will cheer me up if anything will!*

Two hours later Chrissy climbed the hill to their apartment, tired but happy, excitedly carrying a bag from one of the more exclusive stores in the city. She still could not believe her good luck. She had only wandered into the shop to get an idea of the latest styles, but there she had found the perfect dress hanging on a reduced rack, looking like the one swan in a whole lake of ugly ducklings. It was truly a dream dress—made of a silvery gossamer-light fabric with yards of full skirt and a slim, fitted top. When she tried it on, she looked exactly like Cinderella after the magic wand had been waved. All she needed was a pair of glass slippers! And even more miraculous, the wand had been waved over the price, too. It was marked down to half price and Chrissy could just about afford it.

She glanced down into the bag to make sure the dress was real and not just a fantasy.

There it was, still as silky and shimmering as ever, catching the rays of the afternoon sun as she lifted the bodice from the tissue paper.

Maybe this is the turning point, she thought. *So many bad things have been happening to me, maybe this is a sign that everything will start going right from now on.* She ran her fingers over the soft fabric before dropping it back into the bag. *If only Cara and I were still friends,* she thought, her elated mood beginning to fade as she started to climb the steps to the apartment, *because I'm dying to show this dress to somebody!*

She mounted the last of the stairs and put her key into the front door.

"Aunt Edith?" she called hopefully, even though her aunt was rarely home from work this early. "Uncle Richard?" She poked her head around the kitchen door, then tiptoed into her uncle's study. The door was wide open and nobody was sitting at Uncle Richard's messy desk.

"Rats!" Chrissy mumbled. "Then I'll have to phone Tracy and ask her to get over here so that I can show her."

She went down the hall to her bedroom, determined to try on the dress once more, just to make sure there wasn't some reason she hadn't noticed why it was half price, like a missing armhole or a big stain down the back. As she pushed open the door, there was a gasp and whispering silver shimmer as Caroline spun around.

"Oh, Chrissy, I didn't hear you come in," Caroline stammered. "I was just trying on . . ." she broke off as Chrissy gave a shriek of horror. "What's wrong?" she asked, watching Chrissy's face. "I bought a ball dress this afternoon. Don't you like it?"

Chrissy continued to point and stare at the shimmering, silvery miracle which now encased Caroline's body, not her own. She even glanced down at the bag in her hands, half-expecting to see it empty—as if the magic wand might have spirited her dress out of the bag and onto Caroline instead.

"What's the matter, Chrissy?" Caroline asked. "Is there something wrong with the dress?"

"My dress," Chrissy managed to stutter, her face getting hotter and hotter by the minute. "That's my dress you're wearing."

"What do you mean?" Caroline asked in bewilderment. "I just bought this dress at Saks. Imagine that, Chrissy. It was on their reduced rack and it was half price and it's just perfect and . . ."

"And it's my dress," Chrissy yelled, so fiercely that Caroline stopped talking and took a step backward. Chrissy wrenched the bag open. "Look!" she yelled, holding up her identical dress.

"Oh," Caroline managed to stammer. She gave a little giggle. "How funny—at least it shows we've both got the same good taste!"

"But we can't both wear it," Chrissy said, feeling her head boiling up to an explosion point like a steam engine. "We'd look like the Bobsey Twins. You'll have to take it back."

"I'll have to take it back? You've got a nerve, Chrissy Madden. I bought mine first. You'll have to take yours back," Caroline said angrily.

"But it looks perfect on me. It was just the dress I'd dreamed of," Chrissy protested.

"Same for me. It was just the dress I'd dreamed of, too."

"You don't even know who you're going with

yet," Chrissy blurted out. "You haven't even got a date."

"I have, too, got a date, no thanks to you. Some nerve you've got, asking my ex-boyfriend to the ball." Caroline's own voice rose to meet her cousin's. They stood facing each other like two boxers in a ring, just warming up for the fight.

"That's right, your *ex*-boyfriend," Chrissy said, more calmly than she felt. "You can't pretend you have any claim on him right now."

"I have a better claim on him than you," Caroline answered haughtily.

"You didn't even think of asking him until he asked me."

"How do you know what I thought?" Caroline shouted. "You never know what I'm thinking because you're so wrapped up in yourself. Every minute of every day it has to be what little Chrissy wants. I've had to spend two whole years giving in to little Chrissy all the time—giving up half my room, putting up with mess and clutter, never a moment to myself and you following me everywhere breathing down my neck."

"I do not breathe down your neck and I haven't noticed you giving in to me, either."

"That's because you don't notice anything except yourself. Talk about spoiled. Boy—I've never met anybody so spoiled as you!"

Chrissy looked amazed and hurt. "Me? Spoiled? I like that," she said. "You sulk every time I talk to one of your friends or try to join in one of your activities."

"That's just not true."

"It is, too—and what's more, you're jealous of me. You're always trying to compete and do better than me."

It was Caroline's turn to look amazed and hurt. "Like when?" she demanded.

"Like when you decided to enter the speech contest just because I said I was going to enter it."

I did not enter just because you wanted to. For your information, I was planning to enter the contest long before you thought of it, I just didn't blurt it out to the world the way you always do. You flatter yourself if you think I'd want to copy you in anything."

"That's what it looks like to me. You can't stand to see me be in the limelight because you're so wishy-washy yourself!" Chrissy retorted.

Caroline's cheeks were dangerously pink, her eyes dangerously bright. "If I wanted to do something because you did it," she said evenly, "most of the time I'd be wanting to make a giant fool of myself, because that's what you spend most of your time doing."

"I do not!"

"Do, too! Who else would get carried away on a hang glider? And that's only the latest on a long list of dumb things you've done. We'll all be laughing for years over Chrissy the Klutzy Clown!"

"How dare you. I am not a klutzy clown! I'm no more clumsy than anyone else," Chrissy retorted angrily.

"Oh, no? Let's just say that if you wear this dress to the ball, you'll probably put your foot through it and rip it off while you're dancing, and then you'll sit in the punch bowl, and go into the boys' bathroom by mistake. . . ." Caroline started to giggle.

This was too much for Chrissy. With a growl of rage she sprang forward. "I hate you," she yelled, "take my dress off right now before . . ." She grabbed at Caroline, but as Caroline went to move out of her way, Chrissy grabbed her skirt instead. There was a horrible, loud ripping sound and Caroline sat down hard on the floor, leaving Chrissy with a long piece of fabric in her hand.

For a moment neither of them moved, each staring horrified at the other. "My dress," Caroline said softly. "You've wrecked my lovely dress. . . . Chrissy, do you really hate me that much?" She hid her face in her hands, muffling her sobs.

Chrissy was still staring, horrified. Now she dropped to her knees beside Caroline's hunched form and put her hand gently on Caroline's shoulder. "Cara, I'm sorry. I really am," she stammered. "I really didn't mean . . . Cara . . . I didn't mean to . . ." She jumped up and held the fabric up to the dress—"Look, we'll fix it. We'll sew it back together so that nobody will ever notice!"

"You can't sew it back together!" Caroline muttered through her hands.

"Then we'll redesign it—we'll glue it, we'll staple it—you can wear the ripped part as a veil and be mysterious—see?" And she wrapped the fabric around her head so that only her eyes were showing.

Caroline looked up, gave a weak smile and shrugged her shoulders. "Face it, Chrissy. It's ruined," she said. "I should have known it," she went on haltingly. "I should have known that it was too much to dream for. I never seem to get what I want, anyway. I was just plucking up the courage to ask Alex to the ball and you asked him first. Same with the speech. When we first heard about it, I dreamed of entering and you got in first again. Everything I try to do, you spoil it for me. . . ."

Chrissy winced. "Is that what you really think of me?" she asked.

Caroline raised a tear-stained face and nodded. "Not deliberately, I guess," she said, "but you still manage to spoil things. Just because you're you, and I'm me. I dream about things but don't dare tell anyone. It takes me ages and ages to pluck up courage to do things and you hear about them one minute and plunge right in. . . ." she looked at Chrissy shyly. "Miss Peters told me soon after the contest was announced that several teachers thought I'd be a good person to give the speech. At first I took it lightly, but then I decided maybe they were right. I was just plucking up the courage to do it when you came running in, taking it for granted that I'd help you instead. You always take it for granted that I'll drop everything and come running when you need help."

Chrissy opened her mouth to object, then stopped short. Did she really behave like that? Visions of herself rushing in excitedly, calling Cara to help her with ballet or skiing or even Chinese cooking flashed across her mind. Maybe she had used Cara . . .

"If I did, it was only because you know everything about everything and I know nothing," she said at last.

"That may have been true when you first got here, Chrissy," Caroline said, "and I didn't mind helping then, but now you take it for granted."

Chrissy felt her ears burning, this time not with anger but with embarrassment. "Perhaps I have been like that," she said. "But only because you've always been so willing to help."

"I haven't always been willing," Caroline corrected. "But I'm not like you, remember. I have a hard time saying no. You always manage to make me feel so guilty if I refuse."

Chrissy was quiet again. She knew that Caroline was certainly right there, but it didn't feel very good to admit it. "I'm sorry," she said. "It's just that I always seem to be needing help these days."

Caroline looked at her cousin's face. "You don't need any help, Chrissy," she said. "You're doing just fine here."

Chrissy gave a brittle laugh. "Oh sure," she

said, "So fine that I'm probably not even going to graduate."

"What do you mean?" Caroline asked. "Of course you're going to graduate. Everyone graduates—what kind of talk is that?"

Chrissy shook her head slowly. "I'm not joking, Cara. Miss Peters told me that I'm failing government. You know how she never asks to see homework and she hardly ever gives tests. Well, dumb old me thought I could use that period to do my math. Now she tells me that if I don't turn in a completed homework notebook and get a good grade in the final, I won't even graduate."

Caroline's eyes opened wide. "Chrissy, that's terrible."

"So it looks as though you'll only have to compete against Brian Bennet to do the speech," she said quietly. "And you can probably wear my dress. They won't let me go to the ball if I'm not graduating, will they?"

She tried to sound brave but her voice wobbled at the end of the sentence and Caroline moved across to her. "Oh Chrissy," she said gently. "Don't worry. I'll help you pass Government. You have to graduate."

A tear trickled down Chrissy's cheek. Somehow it was harder when Caroline was being so nice. "You just said you're fed up with helping me," she said. "That's why I wasn't going to ask you," she said.

"Don't be ridiculous," Caroline said with a grin.

"You can have my notes. And seeing that I'm the neat one, they are all in order."

"You're being so nice to me," Chrissy said, "when I've just accused you of all sorts of mean things and wrecked your dress."

"I said some pretty bad things, too," Caroline said.

"I guess I deserved them," Chrissy answered. "I have taken a lot for granted—like living in your room and expecting help with everything. I'm sorry. You'll be rid of me soon."

Caroline reached out and touched her cousin's shoulder. "Oh, Chrissy, I don't really want to be rid of you. You've become like a sister to me—I expect that's why were fighting now. All good sisters fight, but they always make up afterward."

The two cousins looked at one another, then enveloped each other in a big hug.

"Oh, Cara," Chrissy said, brushing back tears. "You are very special to me, you know. I've been so miserable while we've been enemies."

"Me, too," Caroline said. "Let's start again, shall we, Chrissy?"

"You bet," Chrissy said. "I don't even care if you win the speech contest and you can even go to the dance with Alex in my dress if you want to."

"Don't be crazy. You don't have to give up everything for me any more than I have to give up everything for you."

"But I insist, Cara," Chrissy said firmly.

"No way!" Caroline said.

Chrissy stared at her cousin, then burst out laughing. "Now we're fighting over being nice!" she said. "But, Cara, I really do wish that you'd . . ."

"Not another word," Caroline said, "Or I'll throw you out of my room. Now, help me get this dress off and let's see if it really is a hopeless case."

Chapter 13

Chrissy sat humming happily to herself as she threaded the needle. The warm sun streamed in through the open window. On the branch of the bougainvillea beneath her window, two mockingbirds were trying to out-sing each other and, a bee was buzzing among the flowers. It was everything that a summer afternoon should be—peaceful, relaxing, happy. Chrissy looked down at the shimmering silver fabric in her hands and smiled at herself. She was actually glad that she had ripped Caroline's dress and insisted that Cara have hers. It was even worth giving up the chance to wear her dream dress to make everything okay with Cara again. Since they had talked things out, they were now back to being best friends. And Cara's government notes were an enormous help, so that was one huge load off her shoulders. Even the dress was not totally ruined. In fact Chrissy had come up with a pretty good idea to make the dress look sensational.

She had been browsing through a teen magazine feature on proms when she saw exactly what she could do to save the dress! One of the models wore a shimmery silver gown just like hers, but draped over the top was yards of swirling blue chiffon so that the silver just peeked through. It looked easy enough to do and Chrissy had gone right out to buy several yards of sheer blue fabric to drape her dress.

She tried on the dress, pinning the full skirt in back to hide the rip. Then she tucked one end of the blue chiffon into the top of the dress and started to wind it around herself, trying to imitate the picture.

"Hey, not bad," she said, surveying the effect in the mirror. The twisted chiffon made the dress look long and slinky, and quite different from Caroline's gown. She gathered her hair and twisted it into a chic bun at the side then sucked in her cheeks like the model in the picture. "Very sexy," she pronounced.

"Chrissy?" Caroline's voice called, "Are you alone in there?"

"Just talking to myself," Chrissy called. "Come and see what I'm doing!"

"I need some help," Caroline called back, "I've got an armful of books and I can't open the door."

"I'll get it," Chrissy yelled back. She tried to

walk toward the door when a serious flaw in her
dress design became obvious. She could not walk
in it. "Coming, Cara," she yelled and, putting her
feet together, she jumped across the floor.

"What was that funny noise—what were you
doing in there?" Caroline asked as Chrissy finally
managed to open the bedroom door.

Chrissy grinned sheepishly. "I was designing a
new dress," she said.

Caroline dumped the books on her desk and
eyed her cousin's creation. "Wow, Chrissy—is
that the dress you ripped? You'd never know, it
looks fantastic."

"There's only one problem," Chrissy said, still
grinning. "Watch." She bounced back across the
floor again like a human pogo stick. "This is the
only way I can move in it."

Caroline started to giggle. "That might be lim-
iting at a dance," she said, "Unless you can convince them that it's the latest dance step."

"I could do that," Chrissy said. "Hey,
everybody—do the Bounce!" she said, bouncing
around the room again.

"There's just one more problem," Caroline
reminded her. "The ballroom is up a long flight of
steps. You'd never bounce your way up all of
those."

"You're right," Chrissy said. "Oh, rats. It looked
so simple, too."

"Why don't we both chip in and buy you a new
dress," Caroline said, "Or you take the silver

dress and I'll get another one. I don't mind, honestly."

"I won't hear of it," Chrissy said, "and I'm not wasting precious money on another dress. I've got the fabric now and I know how I want it to look. I'll just play with it until I get it right."

"That's one of the things I admire about you, Chrissy," Caroline said, perching herself on the edge of her bed as Chrissy began to unwind the yards of blue. "You don't quit. You keep on going until you achieve your goal. I bet that helps you to do well in life."

Chrissy turned away, not wanting Caroline to see her face. She almost felt like crying again. *Maybe sometimes it's better to quit*, she thought, her mind turning to the speech contest. *If it's going to cause more problems between Cara and me, it's not really worth it.*

Out loud she said hesitantly, "About this speech contest, Cara . . ."

Cara made a face. "I hope you are not asking me to help you write your speech, Chrissy!"

"No, of course not." Chrissy paused. "I just wondered if you wanted me to drop out," she finished.

"No way!" Caroline replied firmly. "We'll both work on the very best speech we can and we'll both be proud if the other one wins."

"But what if Brian Bennet beats both of us?" Chrissy asked.

Caroline stifled a giggle. "You're not serious?" she asked. "I mean, Chrissy, I honestly don't see him as a threat to anybody. I can't think who nominated him to be a candidate. It must have been a joke!"

Chrissy smiled. "You're right," she said. "A guy who laughs like a hyena couldn't really be a threat to two bright, witty, smooth young women."

But as they walked together into school on Monday morning, they both paused, open-mouthed, in the front hall. A poster before them read: "Vote for Brian Bennet for Senior Speech. Select the only boy for grad speech. Brian Bennet speaks on the future of the computer—Will they really rule our lives one day?"

Caroline turned to look at Chrissy. "Boy, he's really going out for this in a big way, isn't he?" she asked shakily.

Chrissy nodded, still staring wide-eyed at the posters. "I think maybe you should have encouraged his crush a little more," she said. "If he still worshipped you, he'd never have wanted to beat you."

Caroline shrugged. "There are certain limits," she said. "If I had to choose between being nice to BB and winning the speech contest, I think I'd rather lose."

"But we can't let him beat us," Chrissy said. "Not Brian Bennet. Imagine him giving the speech, laughing like a hyena at his own jokes!" She turned to Caroline. "You don't really think these posters will help him win, do you? I mean, you don't think he's really got a chance, when it comes to making speeches?"

Caroline shifted nervously from one foot to the other. "I don't know, Chrissy. Until now I would have thought he didn't have a prayer, but now I'm not so sure. Publicity is an important factor, you know. Sometimes people get to be president just because they are well known, not because they are the best. And he is speaking on computers. He knows a lot about them . . ." she sighed and pushed back her hair from her face, *"Mon Dieu*, he certainly knows a lot about them. If you ever dare talk to him about them, he'll launch into a monologue on bits and bytes and disks and all kinds of weird things."

"So his speech could be pretty good?" Chrissy asked hesitantly.

Caroline nodded. "It could be, I guess. He's not the world's best personality, but he is an expert on computers. . . ."

Chrissy paused for a moment. "I've been thinking," she said. "Maybe one of us *should* drop out. With two of us, we'll just be splitting the votes and opening the way for Brian Bennet to beat us both." She paused again, as if summoning up a big effort. "Look, Caroline," she said. "You go ahead and give your speech. I mean it this time. Your speech is sure to be better than mine anyway. You stand a much better chance of winning than me."

"No I don't," Caroline answered. "You're much better at speaking in front of lots of people. You put things across so much better. It's okay. I don't mind dropping out to help you win."

"No, I insist," Chrissy said. "I don't want this nearly as badly as you. Besides, it's your school. It's only right that you get to be the one doing the speech."

"But you've had to give up so much," Caroline said forcefully. "You've had to give up your whole senior year back home. It's only right you get to do one special thing here. I don't mind dropping out, honestly I don't."

"But you were really looking forward to this, Cara. I'll drop out. My speech isn't even written yet, anyway."

"Neither is mine."

"But you have better ideas than me."

"The only ideas I can come up with are boring."

"You're being stubborn again!"

"No, I'm not. You are."

Several figures closed in around the arguing girls. They were fighting so loudly that they didn't notice their friends arrive until Tracy stepped between them.

"What's this?" Tracy demanded. "Not fighting again. We thought you two had finally made up."

"I should hope so, after all the trouble we went to," Justine said.

"Yeah," Randy chimed in. "We spent all night making those dumb posters."

Caroline and Chrissy broke off their argument.

"You did what?" Caroline asked in disbelief.

The others looked at each other uncomfortably. "Didn't you know BB was a write-in?" Tracy asked. "Well, we wrote him in."

"You wrote in BB against us?" Chrissy demanded.

"What on earth made you do that?" Caroline asked. "We thought you were our friends!"

The others exchanged looks again.

"We did it because we are your friends," Tracy said, "and we like both of you. We couldn't stand to see you not speaking to each other."

"And your fight was tearing us apart, too," Maria added. "We couldn't help taking sides. You would have broken us up as a group if you'd gone on."

Caroline and Chrissy looked at each other and both blushed at the same time, remembering how childishly they had behaved. They certainly hadn't considered their friends feelings at all.

"We never stopped to think about you," Chrissy mumbled, "and you were right. We were acting like dumb kids."

"It was crazy to get so wound up about a speech contest," Caroline agreed. "In fact we were just having a little friendly discussion about which of us should drop out and let the other one win."

"Is that what it was—friendly discussion?" Justine asked with a raised eyebrow. "We could hear you down on Fisherman's Wharf."

Tracy giggled. "Cara, you've become as loud as Chrissy. You were the quietest person until last year. I'm glad to see you're speaking to each other again. Or rather yelling. . . ."

"Aren't you glad we helped get you back together by writing in Brian Bennet?" Maria asked. "It was my brilliant idea."

"Yeah, thanks a lot," Chrissy said, giving Caroline a quick look.

"But writing in Brian Bennet of all people?" Caroline asked. "How was that supposed to change things?"

Tracy flushed. "We hoped you'd both agree that you'd rather see the other one win than somebody neither of you could stand," she said. "We hoped you'd see how childish you'd been."

"It wasn't easy coming up with a person to nominate," Maria agreed. "We wanted somebody neither of you liked, but someone who wouldn't have a real chance of beating you, either."

"I don't know so much about that," Chrissy said. She let her gaze wander back down the halls. "What about all your posters? You can win anything with enough publicity."

"But Brian Bennet?" Randy asked, starting to chuckle. "Be serious. You could publicize Phyllis Diller for Miss America, but she still wouldn't have a chance of winning."

"But he's going to give a speech on computers," Caroline said, looking up earnestly at Randy. "And that guy really knows his computers. He might impress his audience in a way we never could. We're not experts on anything, Chrissy and me."

"Just in getting along with each other," Maria said with a laugh. "You could give a speech on 'Close Encounters of the California Kind'!"

The loud jangle of the warning bell for first period broke up their discussion. They made plans to meet for lunch, then turned in separate directions.

"I'll see you at lunch, too, okay?" Caroline said to Chrissy.

"Er . . . what?" Chrissy asked.

"Are you having a vision or something?" Caroline said, giggling. "You have the strangest look on your face."

"Cara," Chrissy said slowly, "I think I'm getting a terrific idea! I might not be as brainy as you or Brian Bennet or anyone else in this school, but I think I'm coming up with a terrific, fantastic, incredible idea!"

"About what?" Caroline asked excitedly.

Chrissy's face was becoming flushed with excitement. "About us, and the speech contest! Neither of us has to drop out, Caroline!"

"We'll just shoot Brian Bennet? Great idea! Wish I'd thought of it."

"No, not that!"

"We just lock him in the broom closet until the contest is over? Much less messy. Good idea."

Chrissy grabbed her cousin's arms. "Stop fooling around and just listen," she said. "How about this, Cara. We'll both give the speech!"

Caroline's eyes scanned her cousin's face. "As a duet, you mean? Speaking in unison?"

"No, you dope!" Chrissy was emphatic. "We'll give a joint speech and we'll give it on prejudice. You know how we both had a lot of ready-made ideas about each other when we first met, but we've both had to learn to fit in with new lifestyles. I think kids could learn a lot about prejudice and accepting people who are different just from listening to what we went through!"

Caroline was beginning to smile. "Hey, you know that's not half bad!" she said.

"And we could make it funny," Chrissy added. "Funny speeches always go down better. We'll just put in all the crazy things we did, trying to fit in. You know—like you and the cow you thought was a bull!"

"Let's leave that one out," Caroline said quickly. "How about you getting lost and riding home on the fire engine? Or the first time you ate sushi?"

"How come you remember more things about me than I do about you?"

"Because I don't do crazy things as often as you! What about that tower of soda cans that won the art show?"

"Great—I don't mind you including that. It shows how superficial the values are here," Chrissy remarked.

"They are not!"

"Oh, come on, Cara—you know they are."

"And it's not superficial to win a boy with a pie-baking contest? If anything is primitive, that is!"

They looked at each other, then both burst out laughing.

"I guess we've got plenty of material," Caroline said. "We'd better start working on it in a hurry. We've only got one more day."

"And if we can just get through that without fighting . . ." Chrissy went on.

"We'll have a winning speech!" Caroline finished. "You're a genius, Chrissy. See you at lunch!"

And she ran off, leaving her cousin looking fondly after her. *I'm really going to miss Cara,* Chrissy thought. *She's the best almost-sister in the world. We fight sometimes, but we really belong together!*

Chapter 14

"Are you sure we're going to beat this guy?" Chrissy whispered to Caroline as they walked into the auditorium together. Caroline had been completely silent since they had met by her locker and Chrissy could not tell whether she was extra scared or just trying to get her thoughts in order. Chrissy's own stomach was full of butterflies turning double and triple flip-flops.

The big auditorium seemed to have grown even bigger, with the path down the center aisle now several miles in length. Maxwell seniors and faculty were wandering in from all sides, talking noisily so that their voices echoed back from the high ceiling above.

Caroline glanced back and gave a bright, encouraging smile that didn't fool Chrissy. "No problem," she said. "Look at us—poised, intelligent girls, warm inspiring topic, just enough humor. We can't lose!"

"You really think so?" Chrissy whispered as they reached the front of the auditorium. Up on stage, Miss Peters was sliding the podium to the center of the floor.

"Would you choose us or Brian Bennet?" Caroline asked back.

"Well, I'd choose us, but then I'm prejudiced," Chrissy answered with a grin. "Logic tells me that we can whip the pants off this guy, but I have this horrible vision of BB getting up there and being brilliant—you know, spouting all these impressive facts and figures on computers and bits and bytes and then we get up with our homey stuff and look like fools."

Caroline pushed back her hair nervously. "Well, we can only do our best, Chrissy. It's too late now to change our speech. All we can do is sit back and let BB do his worst and then give it our all."

Chrissy opened her book bag and peered in. "Not quite," she whispered. "I thought I might bring a few props along, just in case . . ."

"What are you talking about?" Caroline asked.

Chrissy lifted a lemon, just high enough for Caroline to see. "You know, stuff like this . . ."

"You're going to use a lemon in our speech as a visual aid?" Caroline asked, looking confused.

"Not in our speech, dummy. In BB's speech. If he's too good, we both start sucking lemons.

Don't you know what that does to a person who watches you? It puckers up their mouth so they can't talk properly."

"Chrissy!" Caroline looked horrified. "Don't you dare! That's sneaky and underhanded and I won't let you."

"Not even if BB's about to win the contest?"

"Not even. Either we win fair and square or not at all. Give me that lemon right now."

Chrissy handed it over. "Spoilsport," she muttered.

"And don't you try any other tricks," Caroline scolded.

Chrissy put on her innocent face, opening her big blue eyes extra wide. "Not even put a whoopee cushion on his chair? Not even tie his shoelaces together just before he gets up to speak?"

"Chrissy!" Caroline said, shaking her head in horror, "You are something else."

Chrissy grinned. "Just making use of my down-home horse sense," she said. "At least I got you to relax, didn't I?" she asked, looking smug. "You were looking all grim and tense as we walked down the hall."

Caroline took her place on a chair in the front row. "You are the world's worst con artist," she said. "You should make a career in politics."

Chrissy smiled sweetly and sat beside her. Miss Peters rapped on the podium with her gavel and called for silence. She spoke for a while about the contest and the high traditions of fine speechmaking and the honor of Maxwell High, then she summoned Brian Bennet to the podium. He was wearing a dark blue blazer and gray slacks for the occasion, and his spiky hair was slicked down as if it was glued to his head.

"Mr. Principal, members of the senior class, faculty," he began, clearing his throat nervously. "Are computers destined to take over a bigger role in tomorrow's society? Is the pocket-sized computer that can pay our bills, regulate our house temperature, order our groceries and check our kids' homework, mere science fiction or just around the corner? Will the superchip open whole new facets of computer design and function?"

Chrissy glanced at Caroline. As Brian warmed to his subject he was sounding more and more confident. He also sounded as if he knew what he was talking about. "I think you'd better give me back that lemon," she whispered.

"Which reminds me:" Brian went on. "Do you know what the big computer said about the PC? He's a microchip off the old microchip!" and he broke into his dreadful hyena laugh. There was a muffled giggle from the audience. Caroline glanced at Chrissy again. This time a triumphant glance passed between them.

After several more very bad jokes and some good information Brian sat down to polite applause and Miss Peters called Caroline and Chrissy to the stage. As if in a daze they made their way up the steps and stood facing a senior class which seemed to have quadrupled in size. Chrissy could feel Caroline standing very close to her, as if she wanted the reassurance of Chrissy's presence. Chrissy took a deep breath and began.

"Prejudice! The dictionary defines it as 'a judgment formed before the facts are known.' We usually think of prejudice as an intolerance or hatred of other races, or religions. Here at Maxwell High we are lucky not to experience much prejudice toward other races or religions. We pride ourselves on knowing the facts. We have spent four years cramming our heads with facts alongside students of many races and religions."

Caroline leaned toward the microphone and took over. "Two years ago I would have defined myself as an enlightened, unprejudiced person, and yet, when my cousin Chrissy first arrived from Iowa, I had her stereotyped before she got off the plane."

Ten minutes later the cousins sat down to a big round of applause. Chrissy looked at Caroline and Caroline looked at Chrissy.

"Do you think we did it?" Caroline whispered.

"Sounded good to me," Chrissy said, "In fact I thought we were fantastic, but then I may be prejudiced."

"I didn't think my knees were going to hold me up that long," Caroline confessed. "They were shaking so hard I thought the audience would hear the rattling over the microphone."

"You didn't come across as nervous," Chrissy

said. "You were as cool and collected as ever. In fact it was you who kept me going. I kept thinking, if she can be so cool, I don't need to get nervous, either!"

Caroline smiled delightedly. "I'll never make it through to the end of the afternoon when they announce the result," Caroline said. "We were better than him, weren't we?"

"Are you kidding? Even a giraffe would have been better than him," Chrissy said, giving Caroline a huge grin, "and anyone who has taken biology knows that giraffes can't even talk!"

People crowded around the cousins to congratulate them, but it was not until the end of the day when they stood in front of the notice board and read: WINNERS OF THE SPEECH CONTEST: C. MADDEN AND C. KIRBY, that the tension of the day finally exploded.

"We did it! We won!" Caroline whooped, dancing around and hugging her cousin and her friends.

"I can't wait to phone home with this news!" Chrissy exclaimed. "Just wait until Tammy Laudenschlager hears!"

They were still dancing about the hall with glee when they heard a stern voice behind them.

"Miss Kirby. Miss Madden."

The girls stopped celebrating and turned around to see their principal looking at them with a scowl on his face.

"Yes, Mr. O'Brien?" they answered together.

Mr. O'Brien's scowl turned into a grin.

"Congratulations, girls," he said, shaking their hands. "Excellent speech."

Chrissy and Caroline grinned back. "Thank you, Mr. O'Brien."

Mr. O'Brien waved his hand. "Don't let me interrupt. Carry on."

When he had disappeared around the corner, the whole group once more exploded into noisy laughter.

"We make a good pair, don't we?" Chrissy remarked to Caroline.

"The best," Caroline replied. "Just make sure you pass that government exam and graduate because I'm certainly not giving that speech alone!"

Chrissy beamed back at her. "Don't worry— wild horses wouldn't keep me away from graduation now."

"I don't think there are too many wild horses in San Francisco at the moment," Caroline teased, then dodged down the steps as Chrissy threatened to grab her.

"Celebration pizza tonight!" Maria shouted after them. "Meet at Pete's Pizza at seven o'clock. Our treat!"

"Sounds great, we'll be there," Chrissy yelled back.

"Trust Maria to arrange a pizza party," Caroline said to Chrissy as they hurried home to change.

Chrissy grinned. "You know Maria—any excuse for an eating binge," she said. "If we'd lost, she'd have arranged a consolation pizza party!"

"We're lucky to have such good friends," Caroline said. "To think that our silly fight almost spoiled everything with them as well. Now we can be back to the way we were and have them around to share our success."

"I still can't really believe it, Cara," Chrissy said. "To think of me—little Chrissy Madden, making that big speech! There's only one thing that means more to me."

"And what's that?" Caroline asked.

"A pepperoni pizza!" Chrissy yelled and broke into a run toward home.

At precisely seven o'clock they met their friends at the entrance to Pete's Pizza. It was an evening of teasing and jokes, basking in the security of knowing that they had won.

Chrissy looked at the laughing faces around the table. Tonight she had laughed right back at the teasing, even trading good-natured insults with Randy. *How different it is when you feel confident*, she marveled. *When you know what you are worth, then teasing can't hurt you. . . .* At last she knew she was as good as any of the kids at Maxwell High. No longer was she just a little country girl who sometimes did crazy things. Now she had proved that she was a serious, dignified person. And in a few weeks she'd be giving a serious, dignified speech in front of three thousand people! A shiver of delight went down her spine. She couldn't wait to get home and write to

her folks about it. *Wait until Tammy
Laudenschlager hears this!* she thought.

She gazed around the room happily, thinking
of all the good things that she almost missed that
were about to happen after all: the senior ball just
a few days away, and then graduation with the
speech and parties, and finally home to see her
folks and her dog and horse and chickens . . .

Suddenly Chrissy gave a start. She stared hard
into the shadow in the corner of the restaurant
wondering if she was hallucinating. Had the
strain of the day gotten too much for her? The
face at the corner table looked suspiciously like
Bart's. Surely there couldn't be two great-looking
guys like him in one town. Then her eyes finally
caught his. He smiled at her in an embarrassed
sort of way and got up.

"Hi, Chrissy," he said, hesitantly. "I stopped by
to see you but your aunt said you'd be over
here."

"Hi, Bart," Chrissy replied uneasily. "I thought
you'd be busy packing. Don't you leave for
Hawaii in the morning?"

He looked down at her, smiling in that special
way. "I'm not going," he said.

"You're not?" It came out as a squeak.

He shook his head, still smiling. "Nah. I've seen
Hawaii tons of times. I decided it would be
boring—all those immature kids at my school
rushing around screaming, getting drunk and
acting like idiots."

"Oh," was all Chrissy could think of saying.

He glanced at the other occupants of the table who were all now watching him and Chrissy with interest. "My car's outside," he said. "Do you want to come for a drive?"

Chrissy desperately wanted to go, but she'd come to Pete's to celebrate with her friends and it just wouldn't be right to leave now.

"Go on," whispered Caroline. "Everyone will understand."

With a grateful smile at Caroline, Chrissy turned to her friends. "Er . . . this is Bart, guys. I um . . . hope you don't mind, but I'll see you all later. Okay? Thanks for the pizza." Then she hurried him out before anyone could say anything.

They climbed into Bart's sports car, with the top down and roared off into the night. It was a mild summer evening and the last remnants of twilight outlined the black hills with soft rose-gold. Chrissy's hair streamed out behind her and the wind felt good—cool but not cold. Once or twice she looked across at Bart, but he seemed intent on his driving. She wanted to say something—anything to make conversation, but she was not sure where to begin. In her head a wild hope was growing that he had given up the chance to go to Hawaii just for her.

They sped up past the traffic on its way north over the Golden Gate Bridge and disappeared into the tree-covered parkland where the Pacific Ocean meets the bay. Here it was dark and silent.

"Are we going anywhere special?" Chrissy asked, trying to sound casual.

Bart flashed her back a grin. "I thought we'd go skinny dipping in the ocean."

"Oh?" She tried not to let her alarm show through.

Bart laughed. "I'm not that crazy, Chrissy! The ocean's freezing up here in the evening! I just felt like driving somewhere private, where we could get away from people."

"Oh!" This time it was accompanied by a sigh of relief.

"I haven't seen you in a while," Bart said, slowing down to a crawl, so that they could hear the roar of the Pacific breakers down below them. "Have you missed me?"

Again Chrissy was not sure what to say. She didn't want to say the wrong thing and blow everything. If she said she'd missed him, he might think she was being possessive, and she knew how he hated to be tied down. If she said she didn't he might think she didn't care.

"I've been kind of busy," Chrissy said tactfully. "Cara and I just won a speech contest. We're going to give the graduation speech."

"That's great. I'm impressed."

There was a silence. Chrissy couldn't shut off her thoughts any more. "So—you decided not to go to Hawaii after all?"

"Yeah, that's right."

"I see."

"It's a shame you're already fixed up with a date for the senior ball now, because I would have been free after all." He paused. "You are all fixed up, right?"

"Right," Chrissy said, then suddenly her eyes opened wide. "Hey, no, wait a minute! Cara can go with Alex and I'd be free to go with you!"

"Would Cara want to go with Alex?"

"Are you kidding? She practically accused me of ruining her life because she wanted to ask him first."

"Is that right? Then that's great, Chrissy!"

He pulled the car to a complete stop beside the road and slid his arm around her. "You know, it's dumb," he said, "After everything I said about not wanting to be tied down. I really resented the thought of someone else going to the ball with you."

"You did?"

"Yeah. I guess I must be getting serious in my old age."

"Right."

"I suppose I shouldn't take things for granted. I should stop to ask you whether you'd rather go to the ball with me than with this Alex person."

Chrissy turned towards him, eyes shining. "What a dumb question," she said. "Of course I'd rather go with you than with anyone else."

Bart smiled happily. "That's great, Chrissy. Now I'm glad I'm not going to Hawaii."

Chrissy gazed at him adoringly. "You gave up Hawaii just to go to the ball with me?"

He gazed back. "What do you think?" he whispered.

"I can't believe it. I didn't think I was that special to you."

"You are very, very special," he whispered, as he pulled her toward him and kissed her warmly. The kiss lasted a long, long time. Chrissy felt as if she were floating far away from the real world. Speech contest winner and Bart's special girl all in one day! She felt as if she was about to burst with happiness!

The ride home was silent, but it was a comfortable silence. Bart had a big smile on his face as he drove, and Chrissy could not stop thinking about the ball. When they reached the Kirbys' apartment house, Bart took her hand and kissed her again.

"I'm looking forward to the ball," he said. "Is it okay if I borrow my Dad's tux? It's a little late to rent one. Oh, and what color do you want your corsage?"

Chrissy's head was swimming with happiness. "Yes, it's okay, and blue," she replied with a grin. "You don't mind going in a foursome with Cara, do you? I sort of promised I would."

"I don't mind," he said, "as long as I get some time alone with you, too. I want to make the most of the time before you slip off to Iowa."

Chrissy shook her head. "I can't believe it," she said. "I keep expecting the good fairy to tell me it's midnight and find myself back inside a pumpkin."

Bart laughed. "You are funny," he said. "And it

would be kind of messy in a pumpkin. All those seeds, you know."

"But it's just like a fairy tale to me. I win a speech contest—little old Chrissy from Iowa, then the most wonderful boy in San Francisco appears and tells me he gave up going to Hawaii just for me. It's almost too good to be true."

Bart coughed at the back of his throat. "Er . . . there is one thing you should know, Chrissy," he said. "I didn't exactly give up Hawaii just for you."

Chrissy's heart plummeted. She should have known. "You didn't?"

"No. I sort of played a little prank and I wasn't allowed to go."

"You did? What sort of prank?"

"I . . . er . . . put padlocks on all the girls' bathrooms at school yesterday. I just wanted to make school more exciting, but I guess I got a little carried away," Bart admitted. "I put a padlock on the ladies' faculty bathroom, too, and they didn't like that much."

Although she was still upset with him, Chrissy couldn't help grinning. "So you're in big trouble?"

"Pretty big. No Hawaii trip. No senior ball."

"So you're only coming to my senior ball because you can't go to yours?"

"Not exactly. I mean, not at all." He squeezed her hand. "Chrissy, I always wanted to go to your ball. It's just that Hawaii would have been a once-in-a-lifetime thing, you know? Now that I can't go, I'm glad that I get to spend more time with you."

She reached to open the door. "I better be going up, Bart."

But he continued to hold her hand. "Chrissy, I meant what I just said about you being special. You are very special to me, and sometimes . . . sometimes that makes me scared." Bart sighed and looked away. "I guess that's why I don't always treat you as well as you deserve. Since my parents decided to get divorced, I've realized that a lot of times good things turn sour, and I don't want that to happen to us."

"You don't have to worry about that," Chrissy said softly.

Bart turned to her. "But I do have to worry. You're leaving in a few weeks, and then what will happen to me? Sometimes I think we should make the most of our time together, and sometimes I think that if I let you go now, it won't hurt so much later."

"How do you feel right now?" Chrissy asked.

"Like I want to make the most of our time together," he answered, squeezing her hand again.

Chrissy smiled and kissed him lightly on the lips. "Me, too."

Chapter 15

"I can't believe it." Chrissy sighed contentedly as she walked home from school with Caroline and Tracy. "In two more weeks we'll be out of high school forever. No longer little immature kids squealing and yelling, but adult college students, spending our days debating such things as the existence of God and the war in Nicaragua."

Caroline and Tracy exchanged amused glances. "Somehow, I can't see Chrissy lounging on a pillow, discussing these earth-shattering issues, can you, Tracy?" Caroline asked.

"Frankly, no," Tracy answered. "Chrissy would say 'You'd better agree with me or I'm going to wrestle you to the ground until you do.'"

"I would not!" Chrissy objected. "Maybe two years ago when I first came here I would have done stuff like that," she said smoothly, "but I've learned a lot, you know. The cultured life-style here has grown on me. Now I am a mature, rational human being, ready to face any situation with calmness. . . ."

They reached the bottom of the steps leading to their apartment building. Caroline reached into the mailbox and drew out a handful of mail.

"Anything for me?" Chrissy asked calmly.

Caroline flipped through it. "Only one from your mother," she said.

Chrissy took the envelope. "Oh great! I can't wait to find out what Tammy Laudenschlager did when she found out that I'm giving the graduation speech. I wonder if she fainted or gnashed her teeth or what."

"Probably fell into a blueberry pie. They seem to do that sort of thing back in Danbury," Caroline said with a giggle.

"Oh, shut up," Chrissy said, giving Caroline a friendly push. "Don't tell me you're not excited about giving the speech. I've noticed how pleased you look when people come up to you in the halls to congratulate you. And you lapped up that interview in the school newspaper . . ." She took the letter out of its envelope and quickly scanned down the page. "Holy Mazoly!" she whooped, loudly enough to echo across the street. Tracy grinned at Caroline. "What was Chrissy just saying about being mature, rational, and calm?"

"Very funny," Chrissy replied good-naturedly,

"Listen to this: We were all so proud when we heard about you giving the big speech. What an honor, Chrissy. We only wish that we could be there to hear you, but the builders are still working like crazy to finish the farm buildings and we have to be around to supervise them. But don't worry, your grandma made sure the whole town knows about you. She told her friends at the church social and pretty soon you were the main topic of conversation. Ben says to tell you he's mighty proud. Apparently Tammy told him that she didn't think it was such a big deal, but he could tell she really was impressed."

Chrissy let out a guffaw. "That says a lot, doesn't it? I bet her face was bright purple."

"You are funny, Chrissy," Tracy said. "Why should it matter to you what someone a thousand miles away thinks? Don't you agree, Cara?" She paused and turned to Caroline who was standing, halfway up the steps, looking at an envelope in her hands.

"What's that?" she asked.

Caroline looked up. Her cheeks were very pink and her eyes very bright. "There must be some mistake," she said. "It's from the Hammersley Foundation. They've just offered me a scholarship!"

"That's wonderful, Cara!" Tracy exclaimed. "See, I knew you'd get one. . . ."

"But you don't understand," Caroline said, her voice quivering. "I didn't even apply to them. I was going to but I chickened out because I couldn't write a good enough essay."

"Cara," Chrissy began hesitantly. "I think I can explain . . . I sent in your application for you."

"You did what?" Caroline's voice rose to a squeak.

"I thought your essay was good enough," she said. "I fished it out of the wastebasket and I copied it over. Then I mailed it."

"Chrissy, you had no right . . ." Caroline began to stammer. "How many times have I told you not to meddle in my things, and how many times have you promised not to?"

"Caroline—this time was different, you had nothing to lose," Chrissy said. "At the very worst, they would not have given you the scholarship. But the worst hasn't happened. You've got the scholarship and now you can go to Colorado and be with Luke!"

Caroline's eyes lit up. "You're right. I can," she said. "I don't believe it! I'm going to Colorado!" She clutched the letter in her hand as she ran up to the top of the stairway. On the landing, she turned around and held the letter up in the air. "Hey world, guess what?" she shouted. "I did it!" Then she let out a loud Indian whoop.

"Whatever you did, do it somewhere else!" ordered mean Mrs. Langdon from her second-floor window.

"What was Cara saying about me?" Chrissy asked Tracy. "Was she teasing me because I was loud?"

"I think she's picked up a lot of bad habits from you," Tracy said as they caught up to Caroline. "I'm really glad for her. It's great to be able to attend the school you really want."

"And to be with the person you really want to be with," Chrissy added.

Caroline looked at them both and brushed away a tear. "Now I'm going to cry like an idiot," she said. "Shut up, you two."

"It's okay. We'll let you cry, won't we, Chrissy?" Tracy said. "We're very happy for you, Cara."

"I've got a great idea," Chrissy said. "What do you say we all go down to Mama's for her famous Earthquake sundae?"

"Chrissy, we've all got to get into prom dresses tomorrow," Caroline said, laughing and crying at the same time. "And yours is just about as skin tight as you can get."

"So—we'll have a minor tremor instead of an earthquake," Chrissy said. "Come on, we'll dump our stuff upstairs and then go straight down to Mama's. After all, we only have two more weeks to do this together."

"But we can't stay long," Caroline protested, following her cousin up the second set of stairs. "We've still got some work to do on the speech."

"And I've still got some sewing to do on my dress," Chrissy said. "I never did finish getting the blue overskirt in place. I just basted it."

"I think you did a fantastic job, don't you,

Tracy?" Caroline asked. "You'd never know it was the same dress."

"Definitely very sexy," Tracy said, "I hope you don't give Alex any weird ideas!"

"Alex?" Chrissy said. "Didn't you know? I'm not going with Alex any more! Bart's not going to Hawaii—he's coming to the ball with me instead."

"When did this all happen?" Tracy asked in surprise.

"Yesterday, when Bart showed up at the pizza parlor," Chrissy said.

"How romantic," Tracy said with a sigh, "and what a cute looking guy, too. I'll be jealous all evening. But what happened to poor old Alex? Did you just dump him?"

"Not exactly. I gave him to Cara," Chrissy said.

"You make me sound like I'm only one stage better than the Salvation Army!" Caroline said indignantly.

"Just kidding," Chrissy said. "Actually it's worked out well all around because he obviously would rather go with Cara. He only agreed to go with me because I asked him first."

"And what about Cara's date—what's happened to him?" Tracy asked. "This sure is getting confusing."

Caroline grinned. "That worked out well, too, because James has just started going with this junior and he really wanted to take her to the ball, but he'd already agreed to go with me."

"So everyone ends up happy," Chrissy said

with a big sigh. "And I get to go with Bart and wear my sexy dress."

"Like I said before," Tracy said firmly, "I hope you don't give Bart too many ideas."

"He already has plenty," Chrissy declared, "but I think I can handle him."

"The old hog-roping trick again," Caroline said laughing.

"That's right," Chrissy agreed, as she unlocked the door to the Kirby apartment. "We certainly do learn some useful things on the farm. But right now I don't want to *rope* a hog—I want to *be* a hog and devour an ice-cream sundae." She dumped her books on the kitchen table. "Mama's, here we come!"

Chapter 16

"Pinch me, I've got to be dreaming," Chrissy whispered to Caroline the following night as they stood together at the top of the staircase and gazed into the Saint Francis Hotel. Chrissy stared at the sophisticated people sitting on elegant brocade sofas, beneath enormous chandeliers. They acted as if it was the most natural thing in the world to be in a fantasy land like this. As Chrissy and Caroline and their dates crossed the front hall, Chrissy noted several curious glances from the people in the lounge and she held her head high. Tonight she was just as sophisticated as they were.

At the entrance to the ballroom she again stood transfixed by the glamor and glitter—the silk-clad walls, the sparkle of the lights on the brass band instruments, the shining expanse of polished parquet floor. *Holy Mazoly!* she said to herself. *This is a whole world away from the senior prom back home!* She imagined herself dancing with Bart in the gym at Danbury High. Hundreds of paper flowers would decorate the room and trays of homemade sandwiches would be waiting on checkered tablecoths while a group of local boys hammered out the latest tunes. With a contented sigh, Chrissy once more gazed around the hotel ballroom. The two worlds were so different that she could hardly believe this one was real.

"Holy cow!" Chrissy exclaimed. "This has to be a dream," she said. "I'm standing here in a lovely dress with a handsome prince beside me in an enchanted palace—and when midnight comes, don't anybody tell me!"

"Well, I'm not driving home in a pumpkin," Caroline said and Chrissy giggled. She couldn't help noticing how happy Caroline looked tonight. All the tension of the past several weeks had vanished from her face and she positively glowed as Alex slipped his arm through hers.

"Will you do me the honor of the first dance, Madame?" he asked her.

"Why certainly, Sir," Caroline replied, her full skirt swishing as they moved off to the dance floor.

Chrissy watched them with a smile. *Even just as friends they make a nice pair. I'm glad I didn't end up spoiling things for them*, she thought. *Besides, I'd rather be here with Bart*, she added to herself. She glanced up at him and met his gaze.

"I can't keep my eyes off you," he said. "You look sensational in that dress. It fits you like a second skin."

Chrissy blushed with pleasure, but she certainly wasn't about to tell Bart that the gown fit her so well because she had literally sewn herself into it. First she had gathered the skirt tightly in the back, this time leaving enough room at the bottom to allow her to walk. Then she had sewn some blue chiffon on top of the silver bodice, waiting until she was in the dress to drape the skirt while Caroline stitched the chiffon to the skirt. The result had been well worth the few pricks with the needle.

Maybe I should be a dress designer, she wondered as she looked at the other girls' dresses and noted with pleasure that hers looked so much better than all the frills and bows.

"Shall we go sit down for a little while first?" Bart asked, taking her arm. "I'm still feeling stuffed from that dinner. The food was pretty good, wasn't it?"

Chrissy nodded. The food had been very good. Unfortunately one of the limitations of sewing herself into the dress was that there was no room for it to expand after a big meal.

"Here's a free table," Bart suggested. "We'd better reserve it for your friends." He steered Chrissy through the dancing crowd toward a table in a darkened corner. "Sit down," he said, politely pulling the chair out for her.

Chrissy looked down at the low, brocade seat on the chair and smiled at Bart. Another feature of her dress had become evident as she'd climbed into the limo earlier that evening. She could not sit down in it. She had draped it so tightly across her hips that it would not stretch enough to let her sit comfortably. She had suffered in the limo, propping herself on Bart's knee in a half-standing position. Fortunately the restaurant had fairly high chairs and she had managed to lean herself against her chair in a half-sitting position. But there was no way she could sink to this low chair.

She gave her brightest smile. "I'd rather dance right away," she said. "You know how I love to dance and this tune is one of my favorites."

"I'd rather sit this one out. We'll dance later," Bart said.

"But Bart, this night only comes once in a life-time. How can we waste it just sitting down?" Chrissy pleaded.

Bart sighed but allowed himself to be led onto the floor. "You're a slave driver, you know that," he muttered, but he started dancing and Chrissy noted that he danced well.

The number ended and the band switched to an up-tempo number. Bart looked as if he was about to flee but Chrissy grabbed him and waved to her friends. "Let's all dance in a big group," she called and began to do a wild shake to the beat. Soon her friends were all around her, laughing and flinging their arms wildly.

"This is like some primitive tribal ritual," Bart yelled over the music.

"Yes, don't you love it?" Chrissy yelled back.

Then, from the fast number, the band switched into a slow dance. Couples melted into each others arms.

"Now, this is more my style," Bart said, drawing Chrissy toward him. They began to sway across the floor, his arms tightly around her, his cheek against hers.

"This is just perfect," she murmured back. "I could stay like this all night."

They moved around the floor to the throbbing beat. Chrissy closed her eyes and felt she was floating on a cloud of happiness. *I'll remember this moment forever,* she decided.

Suddenly she was shaken out of her reverie by a tap on her shoulder.

"Chrissy," Caroline whispered in her ear.

"Not now," Chrissy whispered back. "Can't you see I'm busy?"

"But listen," Caroline insisted. "I've got to talk to you."

"When the number's over," Chrissy hissed. Bart had opened his eyes, too, and was staring at Caroline suspiciously.

"When the number's over may be too late," Caroline whispered back urgently. Chrissy caught the urgency this time. "What's wrong?" she whispered.

"Your dress," Caroline answered in a low voice just loud enough for Chrissy to hear. "Bart stepped on it, I guess, and now it's coming unraveled."

"It's what?" Chrissy controlled her shriek at the last moment. She glanced down at her feet to see a large pool of blue chiffon collecting there. "Holy cow, I'd no idea," she whispered. "What am I going to do?"

"What are you girls whispering about?" Bart interrupted, drawing Chrissy close to him. "I thought you wanted to dance, Chrissy."

From the corner of her eye, Chrissy could see Alex, his eyes twinkling with amusement through his glasses. He must have noticed what had happened to her dress. Chrissy hoped no one else had noticed.

"Help!" Chrissy mouthed as Bart began to draw her away from Caroline. Blue chiffon lay behind her like a train, but Bart had closed his eyes again and did not appear to notice anything was wrong. Other couples were moving in. Any moment now someone would step on the fabric, there would be a large ripping sound and it would all be over! As if in answer to Chrissy's worst fears, the band switched to a livelier tune and the couples around them began to jump and stomp in time to the music.

Caroline acted swiftly. She bent to pick up the fabric then wound herself in toward Chrissy, with Alex right beside her.

"What's happening?" Bart asked.

"New dance. Called the Huddle. Haven't you heard of it yet? You get in a foursome and link shoulders like this, just like a football huddle, then you move across the floor. . . ." Caroline said, steering their group toward the exit to the powder room.

"Sounds pretty strange to me," Bart remarked, rolling his eyes at Chrissy, as if to say he didn't know her cousin was so crazy. "And it doesn't look like it's catching on here either," he added. Nobody else is doing it."

"Ah, well Alex picked it up in New York," Caroline said. "It hasn't got here yet. We're introducing it."

They reached the doorway.

"Oh—the music's stopping, what a pity," Caroline said. "Why don't you and I slip to the powder room now that we're here, Chrissy?"

"Good idea," Chrissy said. "See you guys in a minute," and they both fled down the hall.

"You saved my life," Chrissy said, half giggling, half horrified. "One step on that and my dress would have been sitting around my ankles."

They reached the powder room and paused to catch their breath. "The Huddle," Chrissy said, giggling with relief. "You're getting as crazy as me for coming up with weird schemes, Caroline."

"I've had a good teacher for two years," Caroline said. "Now, let's see what we can do with you."

Chrissy stood very still as Caroline wrapped the blue chiffon around her in an attempt to make the dress look the way it did before. "I've only got one small safety pin," Caroline said, "So I don't think you'll be able to move much again—not without disaster striking, that is."

"You're a genius," Chrissy said, admiring herself in the full length mirror. "It looks almost like a dress again. At least in this dim light I should get away with it."

"Just remember there's only one small pin holding it," Caroline warned again as they made their way back to the boys. Bart was looking somewhat confused and not very happy at being deserted so early in the evening.

"What new delight have you girls planned for us now?" he asked. "The Can-Can? The Thermonuclear War?"

"I'm thirsty," Chrissy said, smiling at him. "Why don't we go get something to drink?"

"Good idea," Bart agreed. "It's hot in here."

They made their way over to the punch table and stood in a darkened corner sipping ice-cold strawberry punch.

"I suppose you are ready to go back for more dancing now?" he asked with a resigned look as they put down their glasses.

"Er . . . I think I've had enough dancing for a while," Chrissy said. "Maybe a slow dance toward the end. . . . How about if we go line up for pictures?"

"Okay," he said, smiling again now. "Good idea, before we start to look too untidy."

They joined the line in a downstairs hallway. Finally it was their turn and Chrissy was careful to pose in such a way that her dress would look all right as they had their picture taken. Afterward they strolled together down the deserted hallways, Bart's arm around Chrissy's waist.

"Chrissy—let's not go back to the others yet," Bart said as Chrissy was about to climb the stairs to the ballroom. "Why don't you and I go upstairs?"

"We are going upstairs," Chrissy said, confusion evident in her voice.

Bart smiled at her. "I mean all the way upstairs. There's a great view from the top of the hotel."

"So I heard." Chrissy stepped back from the sweeping staircase. "I'd love to see the view, but I don't want to miss too much of the ball."

"Don't worry," Bart replied, "just a quick look and we'll go back." He took her hand and led her along the plush carpet to the row of elevators. Confidently, he pressed the button.

They climbed in, whooshing silently upward in a glass tube on the outside of the tower, while the city spread out before them in a glittering landscape. The doors opened again on the twenty-ninth floor and Chrissy followed Bart into a deserted hallway.

"See—wasn't it worth the ride?" Bart asked. "And there's a view at the end of this hallway that looks out on the Bay Bridge. It's gorgeous."

Hand in hand they made their way down the hall past several rooms with closed doors, and around the corner to where the corridor stopped.

At the very end was a small window, only about one foot square.

Chrissy peered out at the view. "Oh Bart, it's fantastic!" she exclaimed. "You were right. I bet this is the best view in the entire hotel."

"Yeah, not bad, huh?" He smiled shyly as she turned to look at him. "My dad was staying here until last week. He's got his own apartment now."

"Oh, Bart," Chrissy said again. "That's too bad. You must miss him."

Bart shrugged. "Well, that's life, isn't it? Anyway, I visited him here a few times last week. That's how I know about this window. My Dad's suite was down the hall we've just come from."

Chrissy just nodded. She wanted to take his hand or give him a comforting hug or something, but he had such a bitter look on his face that she hesitated. *Why am I so nervous?* she wondered. *This is sweet wonderful Bart I'm with, and he's hurting right now. He needs to know that I care.* Tentatively, Chrissy reached for his hand.

"I don't want you to leave, Chrissy," he said in a quiet voice. Then without warning, he wrapped her in a strong embrace and kissed her.

Chrissy closed her eyes and kissed him back. She didn't want to leave him, either, but in the back of her mind she knew that theirs wasn't a lasting relationship.

She pushed him away lightly. "Bart, someone might see us. I don't think they expect this sort of behavior at the Saint Francis."

"The hallway is deserted. Don't worry so

much," he said, leaning down to kiss her again.

"I still feel funny," Chrissy insisted, taking half a step back. "Why don't we go back to the ball?"

Bart looked disappointed, then a gleam appeared in his eye. "I have a better idea. Why don't we get a room here? It will only take a minute to go down to the reservations desk," he suggested.

"A room? Here?" Chrissy squeaked.

"Sure. That way we won't have to worry about anyone seeing us."

Chrissy pulled away from him. "Look, I like you, Bart, but I don't love you," she stammered. "And I'm certainly not ready to make a commitment to you or anyone. Besides, I'm going back to Iowa soon, remember?"

"That's all the more reason," Bart said with a short laugh. "No strings attached that way."

She couldn't believe what she was hearing. Chrissy stared at Bart, taking in his dark hair, always neatly in place; his lively eyes, now hard and serious; and the scowl where his smile usually was. Taking a deep breath, she said calmly, "Bart, you are out of your cotton-pickin' mind. I'm going back to the ball before I lose my temper."

And she stomped off around the corner and down the long hall to the elevator. She heard footsteps behind her, but didn't turn around. *The view was nice, but certainly not that nice,* she thought with a shaky laugh.

On the elevator, Chrissy and Bart stayed in

opposite corners. Bart spent the twenty-nine floors trying to apologize, while Chrissy gazed down at the bright lights of the city, trying to sort out her feelings. By the time the doors opened on the first floor, her anger was subsiding. Although her opinion of Bart had changed dramatically in the past twenty minutes, she didn't want to end the evening in a fight. She wanted to go back to the ballroom and enjoy the rest of the ball.

Bart stepped out of the elevator and reached out his hand to Chrissy. "Friends again?" he asked.

She accepted his hand in answer, but as she went to follow him, she stopped short with a yelp.

"Oh, come on, Chrissy," he pleaded. "I said I'm sorry. I don't know what came over me."

"It's not you I'm worried about," came her strangled answer. "My dress just caught in the elevator door!" Chrissy stood very still while three yards of blue fabric stretched between herself and the closed elevator.

Bart began to laugh. "Finally I've got you well and truly trapped," he said.

"It's not funny," Chrissy said indignantly. "Now help me get out of here before something terrible happens and my dress gets ripped right off me."

"That might be worth sticking around for," Bart said, with a grin.

"Bart Reed," Chrissy said very firmly, "If you know what's good for you, you'll help me get out of here!"

"Okay," he said, still giggling, "I'm calling the

elevator, just be patient, stop pulling like that or the dress really will come off."

At last the elevator arrived. "Thank heavens," Chrissy sighed, "Freedom at last." The doors opened. "It's caught on something," Chrissy yelled. She tried to yank it clear. There was a ripping sound as part of her skirt came away and she went flying into Bart's arms.

"I knew one day you'd come to your senses,'" he teased.

Chrissy could feel the heat rushing to her cheeks. With all the dignity she could muster, she extracted herself from Bart's arms. "Well, shall we go back to the ball?" she asked.

Chapter 17

"I can't believe it. You're really going," Caroline said mournfully as she looked around the room she had shared with Chrissy for the past two years. Chrissy's side of the room—usually buried under a jumble of clothes—was now bare of everything except a stripped bed and an empty chest of drawers.

"And I can't believe I actually got all my stuff into two suitcases," Chrissy said, shaking her head with a pang of regret as she, too, looked around the room. It already looked like Caroline's room again, as if she had never been there.

"You didn't fit everything," Caroline laughed. "You're forgetting about the big boxes we sent by UPS."

"Oh, those few books," Chrissy said. "I never thought I'd be the type of person who'd want to collect books. My brothers will have a fit when they see what I've brought back. They hate reading. I'll have to try and convince them that they won't get anywhere unless they read more . . ."

She was talking brightly, fast and furiously as always when she was under stress, trying to hide from Caroline how painful the parting would be for her.

"Did you leave a book out to read on the plane?" Caroline asked.

Chrissy reached into her flight bag and brought out a large hardcover book called *San Francisco: City of Dreams*. "I've got this one that Aunt Edith and Uncle Richard gave me. There are some great pictures in here of the hilly streets and the Bay and the Golden Gate Bridge. See?" She leaned over to show Caroline a picture of the Bay. "Not as good as the real thing, though," she said wistfully. She put the book back in her bag and got up to gaze out the window. The Bay was especially beautiful today—sparkling blue in the sun.

"Are you okay?" Caroline asked, coming round to stand beside her cousin.

"Chrissy took a deep breath. "I have a horrible feeling I might start crying any minute. It's just really hit me that we won't be together any-more, ever. We'll see each other from time to time and I'm sure you'll be visiting a certain boy in Danbury, but it will never be the same, will it?"

"No, it will never be the same," Caroline said. "No more clothes over my bed and nobody always raiding the refrigerator and asking me to do homework for her . . ."

"If that's how you feel," Chrissy said huffily, "maybe it's a good thing I'm going."

"Chrissy—you know how I feel," Caroline said gently. "I'm going to lose the only sister I've ever had. Nobody will ever take your place. These last two years have been so special—really they have."

"Now you've done it," Chrissy said, putting a hand up to wipe the corner of her eye. "You've started me crying and once I start, it's hard to get me to stop. How do you think the Mississippi River got so big?"

"You dope," Caroline said, giving her a friendly push as she brushed away her own tears.

"Do you think you will be stopping by in Danbury this summer?" Chrissy asked. "Just to drop in on good old Luke, even if you don't want to see me."

"You know I want to see you, Chrissy, but I don't know," Caroline said. "It's all a question of money, isn't it? And I'll be seeing Luke in Colorado in the fall, which is only less than three, glorious, wonderful months away."

"And I'm in for a real exciting summer, helping with the harvest and then I'll be having a blast at good old Iowa State and coming home on week-ends for a real fun time of canning and preserving," Chrissy said flatly.

Her cousin slipped an arm around her shoulders. "Oh, Chrissy, I'm sure you'll have a great time, too."

"But it won't be the same as going *away* to college," she said. "And it doesn't feel the same as knowing you chose your college and your college chose you. I'm only going there because I didn't get in anywhere else."

"You're still on the waiting list for Colorado, Chrissy," Caroline reminded her. "You never know. Besides, Iowa State is a good school."

"But it's so close to home," Chrissy said. "And I'm so scared that I'll find the attitudes narrow and boring after what I've been through here."

Caroline raised an eyebrow. "I thought you would have welcomed down-home attitudes after that little scene with Bart at the senior ball," she said.

Chrissy shrugged. "I handled that okay, I think. Bart just had to learn that he can't get everything he wants." She paused thoughtfully. "I wonder if good old Ben will show any interest this summer? I'm kind of looking forward to seeing him again."

"They say absence makes the heart grow fonder, don't they?" Caroline said with a smile.

"I wouldn't even mind letting him take me to some parties and things," Chrissy went on, "Unless, of course, Tammy Laudenschlager has him hog-tied by now."

"I thought you'd stopped feeling threatened by

her since you gave the graduation speech. I'm sure our speech must have been better than hers!"

Chrissy's eyes lit up at the memory of it. "Ours was sensational, wasn't it? I still lie in bed at night and picture all those strangers, standing around me—little old me—and telling me how deep and meaningful our speech was. And even our picture in the *San Francisco Examiner*. Wait till Tammy sees that!" She turned to Caroline and giggled. "I do feel kind of bad for Tammy though. Mom says her speech was not received too well because she talked a lot about feminist ideas. You know how Danbury men like their women—tied to the kitchen sink."

Caroline laughed. "I can't see you ever tied to the kitchen sink, Chrissy. Or me, either, if I ever get as far as marrying Luke."

Chrissy's eyes glowed as she looked at Caroline. "Wouldn't it be neat if one day you and Luke came and lived right down the road from me and we'd visit every day and our kids would grow up together . . . ."

Caroline shook her head. "That's too far into the future for me, Chrissy. Let's just get through college first, and decide what we want to do with our lives. We can't do everything together or we'll get on each other's nerves too much."

"Me, get on your nerves?" Chrissy asked in mock surprise. "Never! The other way around, maybe. . . ."

Caroline grinned. She knew Chrissy was only

kidding. "I'll really miss having someone around to make me laugh like—"

Down below a car horn honked. The girls looked at each other. Without a word they threw their arms around each other and hugged tight. Chrissy couldn't stop the tears now as she clutched her cousin. The horn honked again.

"Sounds like Daddy is getting impatient," Caroline said, sniffling. "You know how he likes to be on time for everything. We'd better get going."

She led the way out of the room. Chrissy picked up her flight bag, then turned and looked back. "Goodbye, room," she said softly. "Goodbye, Golden Gate Bridge and San Francisco Bay and Fisherman's Wharf and Mama's Sundaes and Pete's Pizza." She paused to wipe a tear away. "And goodbye, dear, sweet Cara," she whispered. "I'll never forget these last two years. I'm going to miss you."

With one last look at the room, Chrissy followed Caroline down the stairs.

After graduation from Maxwell High, Chrissy and Caroline part for the first time in two years when Chrissy returns to Iowa. Don't miss . . .

**SUGAR & SPICE #15:
HOME SWEET HOME**

ABOUT THE AUTHOR

Janet Quin-Harkin is the author of more than forty books for young adults, including the best-selling *Ten-Boy Summer* and *On Our Own*, its sequel series. Ms. Quin-Harkin lives just outside of San Francisco with her husband, three teenage daughters, and one son.